Divided Secrets

R.J. Austin

Printed in the United States

Copyright © 2014 Limon Publishing

ISBN- 978-0692243794

- 2 –
Chapter 1

It was humid and sticky when Alicia stepped out of her nice cool jet-black limo. The driver had been hired to pick her up at the San Cristobel airstrip at exactly 11:00 am and he had been late. Punctuality was not something that she saw as being negotiable. Alicia was not a patient person when it came to the people that worked for her; actually, she was not patient with anyone. Maybe that is why she was here at this beautiful island of the Galapagos all by herself.

Alicia stepped out into the humid hot air and looked up at the blazing sun above her. All she could think about was getting into her room and taking a nice bath to rinse off all the heat of the day. She was accustomed to being in different climates due to the constant traveling her job required and she adapted well, but she did not always have to like it!

"Alicia Valamos" she said hurriedly, "I need to check in"

The hotel lobby receptionist, a young timid woman with deep brown eyes and olive toned skin no more than twenty could not work fast enough for Alicia who was getting more irritated by the minute. To be a relatively small town the hotel was quite amazing, and the staff was very efficient. That is if you asked anyone else besides Alicia.

"It is too much to ask to be in my room within the hour??"

The young girl behind the desk smiled politely and handed Alicia her room card.

" you will be in room 4230 Miss. Valamos." Motioning to the young man smiling by the end of the big marble counter, "This is Luis, he will take your bags up for you, is there anything else I can do for you?"

"No thank you."

Luis was a young man about 20, from what Alicia could tell, he was tall and lanky although she did not pay him much attention. You had to possess some type of importance about you to get Alicia Valamos's attention and you had to have a great deal of power and money to keep it. She stepped into her room and put her Prada handbag and laptop on the etched glass table in the massive area by the big glass doors leading to the private terrace of her suite, while Luis put her bags in the bedroom.

"Did you need anything else Miss. Valamos?"

"No that will be all"

Slipping him a 20, "

Actually you can bring me a map of the islands, and…. where can I find Mathew Black?"

"There is a map of the islands on your bed side table and you can find Mathew down by the docks."

"Thank you."

Alicia had lived most of her childhood in London where she was born although she doesn't remember much, her parents died when she was very young and she went into a foster care system. She has been in Greece at the Animal Research Institute for the last 10 years. Studying animals in their environment has sent Alicia all over the world, at 35 Alicia has been in more countries than most people visit in a lifetime. Living out of hotels and suitcases fits Alicia, she does not like forming ties with people. To Alicia forming ties just means messy endings because in her experience everything always ends... eventually. What better way was there to cleaning up an emotional mess than not to have one at all? At least that was the line she told anyone who had ever stuck around long enough to ask, in the back of her mind she always hoped to find someone someday, but she never put to much stock in that fantasy. After all that is all it was to her was a fantasy, how could anyone fall in love and never get their heart broken? She had her occasional toys here and there but never anything that lasted more than a couple of months or so. Alicia could never quite imagine herself settling down to a family life, at least not a conventional one. Sometimes she would have dreams about her version of the perfect relationship. He would be of her prestige of course, having his own wealth and his heart would be all hers. They would travel the world together, so he would have to have a similar career to hers and there would be passion, passion no-other could imagine.

As soon as Luis left, Alicia went into the bedroom and started unpacking her bags. There is no telling how long I am going to be here she thought, at least the scenery was nice and the weather didn't seem to be too bad, although it was rather humid and she had been told that it sometimes got very cold at night, but she was prepared as always. She would go exploring the surroundings after dinner, which would give the sun time to fall down some making the temperature easier to deal with. Alicia let down her long soft waves to hang down her back, she slipped out of her tailored blue silk suite and jimmy choo pumps and turned on the shower. The cool marble felt good on her bare perfectly manicured feet, it was enclosed with glorious glass doors and big enough for four people with two water spouts one on either side. The hot water felt amazing, pulsating on her tired muscles, from sitting on the plane for so long. The hot water ran from the top of her head down her full perfect breasts, making its way to her firm round bottom and long muscular yet feminine legs. Alicia was in great shape and it showed with every move she made. She washed her long hair with an expensive shampoo that made her smell like jasmine, the suds rushing down her backside. Once out of the shower she wrapped herself in a plush white towel and went into the bedroom sifting through her clothes to find the perfect ensemble to wear to dinner and to explore the downtown area of San Cristobal. She settled on a Soft pink thigh skirt, a white cotton tank and her favorite walking sandals. She slipped on a pair of silk high cut panties and bra to match and then her clothes.

The hotel room was done in shades of beige and lavender and smelled of exotic flowers native to the islands. There was a wide fireplace on one wall in the bedroom, witch she would not be using given the time of year and temperature outside. Too bad, it was amazing she would have to come back here in the cooler, season and take holiday; it was proving to be very relaxing here. The sitting room had two large glass sliding doors leading out onto a terrace that belonged to her room alone with a view of the bay. The warm tropical breeze flowed through sending aromas from the flowers below. The scents in the room matched that of Alicia's hair and her own feminine scent of her soft creamy olive toned skin. Most people that meet Alicia thought of her as the type that would scream at the thought of breaking a nail. Which could not be further from the truth, she was and had always been outdoorsy and willing to jump in whatever came her way, but she also did not see a reason why she could not be both. She loved her designer clothes just as much as she enjoyed her hiking boots and t-shirts. Everyone at the Institute knew Alicia would get down and dirty with the best of them, but outside of her work associates, she was seen completely different. Although Alicia seemed much pampered, she had a rough side to her. She was a researcher and was here to visit the island of Darwin and study the matting habits of the native animals, but not today, she was going to meet with Mathew her guide and then have an early dinner and work on her maps that she would be using the next couple of weeks on the island. Her equipment would arrive tomorrow on the cargo plane and she would have all the technology she needed to feel

completely comfortable in this beautiful
wilderness.

Alicia left the room on her way downstairs to the
lobby to go and find her guide Mathew. The hotel
was a rich array of colors and flowers cascading on
every open ledge in every room. The lobby had an
open veranda at the rear with tropical style patio
furniture and more perfume-filled flowers. The
view was that of the Ocean and white beaches. The
sun had gone down some and the temperature was
a perfect 80 degrees with a light breeze. Alicia sat
in one of the plush chairs facing the water and was
startled when the waiter made his presence known.
"Excuse me; can I get you anything mam?"
"Yes actually I would like a bottled water thank
you."
 She turned her attention back to the water and
pulled her binoculars out of her purse. She looked
out across the water to see a distant island. It
seemed to be covered very densely in lush green
vegetation. The waiter gave her the water and
retreated out of sight, it was nice out here she
thought. There was very little tourist on this island
because of the extreme weather this time of year.
She was not the only guest in the hotel but one of
very few. It was a grand hotel with every amenity
available, heated pool, spa, full exercise room, and
a five star restaurant tucked away on the back of

the third floor with a perfect view of the ocean and surrounding islands. She headed out of the hotel to the street and to her surprise found that the docks were not far and she could walk the short distance there to meet Mathew.

Mathew was an island native; he had hair the color of dark chocolate. It was thick wavy and untamed. His skin was the color of Carmel and his eyes were green like the purest sea. Mathew was average height yet there was nothing average about this native. His chest and shoulders were defined as was his arms and legs; he was a perfect specimen of a man. The fact that he was 32 and single did mean that she could take the pleasures of looking. Alicia tried to make sure she knew her guides very well before meeting them, at least what you could know off paper anyway. She did not like surprises. Alicia just stood there for a couple of minutes taking in his beauty, witch did not happen very often for her. He was bent over some type of chest with fishing gear wearing nothing but a pair of denim shorts that fit his backside to well for her comfort. Alicia did not like the fact that this man took some of her composure away, she did not like to feel out of control even if it was very slight. Mathew had been a guide to the wilds of the Galapagos Islands for eight years now; he loved the freedom it gave. He was amazed at the different people he had met and the sheer excitement of going where very few humans had gotten a chance to go, he loved seeing sights that were only in picture books for most of the world.

Mathew was deep in thought going over a manifest getting ready for the next days shipment of equipment that would be coming in for his next guiding assignment. He was expecting this was going to be a long couple of weeks considering what he had heard about his client. Alicia Valamos. She was said to be very demanding, harsh, and impatient. He liked to kick back and enjoy his work, not be dictated too. Mathew had just sat his manifest to the side and was loading his boat with a few things when he heard someone walk up behind him.

Alicia cleared her throat to gain his attention, when he turned to face her he gave her the brightest devilish grin she had ever seen. Damn everyone had said how uptight she was they never said that she was total knockout.

"Excuse me are you Mathew Black?

"Yes that would be me, you must be Alicia right?

"Yes, what time are we leaving tomorrow to go to Darwin?"

"Well as soon as you would like to leave is fine, I'm finishing up the preparations now."

"Would you like to come on board?"

"No thank you, will you have plenty of room for my equipment, it comes in tomorrow by cargo plane?"

"I'm making preparations for it now, how much is there?

"A few crates and a tree shelter to put together."

Alicia was always well prepared on her trips, she always done her homework and made arrangements to bring the right accommodations for her to observe her interest.

"Yeah I can handle that, lets say we leave about 9am, the cargo plane usually lands around 6am that will give us time to get your equipment loaded and take off before the heat of the sun gets un-bearable."

"Ok I will meet you here tomorrow morning thanks."

Alicia turned away then and started to walk toward the street she had come from. He watched her leave and could not believe how erotic it was just to watch that woman walk, the gentle sway of her very curvy hips, and the long stride of her legs and wow did she have a rack. Mathew always thought of himself as a sensible guy when it came to women and never looked twice at his clients but damn, he could not keep his eyes off of her. She smelled so good and it was hard to keep his sanity while she was near him. He shook his head and headed back to the boat, what am I gonna do with this one?

Alicia fallowed her maps and went exploring the little shops down the main street in front of the hotel, there was a couple of quaint shops she had heard about and really wanted to look in to see if she could find some shoes native to the area that would work with the terrain of the island. She saw a shop across the street called island treasures and she headed straight for it. She looked around but didn't see anything interesting and then an older woman came out of the back that was hidden by a beaded make shift door.
"Hello honey can I help you?"
"Well actually can you tell me where I might find some all terrain shoes, I am going to Darwin tomorrow."
"Oh why yes dear we have that kind of stuff in the back, usually only natives want those items. We keep the tourist stuff in the front, not that we get many in this season.
 Why are you going to the islands? You do know its hurricane season don't ya honey?"
"Yes, but that is the best time of year to catch the penguins and other wildlife in their mating rituals. I am here for animal research."

"Oh well I guess that makes sense then. Here we go how about these, what size do you need?"

"I wear a size 6 and a half please thank you."

 The little woman left to the back, she was short with a thick body structure, she had very sweet eyes and a bun of light brown mixed with some white pilled high on the top of her head. When she came back through the back door, she was carrying a pair of brown ankle leather boots,

"Here honey try these on for size"

"Thank you, Alicia put the boots on and they fit nicely, just a little loose but the thick socks that would be needed at the island would make them a perfect fit."

 The sales lady came up behind her

    "Well, those fit for ya?"

 "Yes maim thank you."

 "Yeah they should work well for ya they are cold resistant and water proof, and no calling me mam I'm Gran to everyone on this island."

"Ok thank you I will need a waterproof light jacket as well please just something to keep the bugs and water off."

 "Oh honey you will need a little more than that its nice outside during the day and not so bad at night here on the main island but out on Darwin it gets mighty cold when the sun goes down. Here try this one it should work for ya.. It has a pull out lining so you can use it during the day and at night, it's also waterproof."

"Ok that will be fine thank you and if you would ring me up please."

Alicia thanked Gran as a local came through the door, she left the little shop and made her way back out into the street.

Chapter 2

Alicia liked the quietness of the island; it was nice to be able to hear her own thoughts for once. Usually she had so many assistants and handlers to deal with even the quietest places seemed very loud and crazy. She had told her research development leader that she came by herself this time or she would gladly stay at home, I guess she was using this trip as a sort of vacation along with the work. Alicia loved to take walks by herself just to think and refocus her energy. It was a rejuvenating process for her that she had used as far back as she could remember, but that was another story all together. Her memory only went back to her teenage years; she could not or would not remember her childhood after her parents had died. She was only four at the time and she had no other family. She was put into the foster care system and had never been adopted or had a real family to call home. She had not thought about what had happened in that one foster home in a long time and still would not go completely back there to those memories. She had thrown herself into her studies, even as a young child all Alicia could think about was getting the very best education she could get so that one day she would leave all that behind and make a living on her own so she didn't have to depend on anyone ever again. She smiled inwardly to herself then, knowing that she had made it. She made a comfortable living doing what she had a passion for. She felt she was one of the lucky ones; she had a foster sister that went through the same things she had as a child and just wished that she knew if she was ok. Katie was 2 years younger than she was and was the epitome of a girly girl; she was always looking up to Alicia even when they were very young. I guess you could say that through all the years of foster care she had a family and that was Katie, she had never thought of her that way before. Something about this island had made Alicia start thinking of the past and remembering images of her and Katie, a couple of the bad ones too. Maybe that is why she had always felt so alone yet ok, she knew Katie was out there somewhere she just hoped that she was ok. She had to stop thinking and get back to the hotel, the sun had fallen for the day and the moon hung low still moving up in the sky to take its rightful place among the million stars that hung there. Absentmindedly she rubbed her hands up and down her arms as she walked towards the hotel; Gran had been right about the cool nights. As she made her way down the street a deep voice stopped her

abruptly with shock and as she turned around to see
who it was she slowly recognized the voice of
Mathew Black. She did not frighten easily but with
all the memories that had come forward in her
mind tonight, she was a little out of her element.
 "Hey sorry I didn't mean to startle you, I was at
the pub across the street fixing to catch a late
dinner and saw you walking alone, have you had
dinner yet?"
 Mathew would have tried anything to get close to
that body. For some reason he had not been able to
shake the picture of her walking away from him on
the dock earlier that day. He did not like the feeling
of her walking away from him, but he liked to
watch her. Why was he even contemplating getting
this woman in his bed, after all she was a client?
What was he thinking??
 "Actually, I had planned to eat earlier but took a
walk and I guess I lost track of time."
"Well, would you like to join me?" His gut told
him not to ask but he couldn't stop himself some
how.
 As soon as he made the offer, her eyes flashed a
glimpse of what he thought was fear and he quickly
added that they could talk about the trip and seal
away the last details while they had dinner. She
seemed to let go of the tenseness she had just felt
and agreed. It was an unusually cool night on the
mainland and the tables to the pub were all outside,

Mathew put his jacket around her and she thanked him, she was more comfortable in it. He ordered for them as they talked lightly about the cargo plane to arrive in the morning and what necessary items they would be taking with them. She was quiet through most of the meal and then he ordered them both a glass of wine.

Alicia thought that Mathew didn't seem like he had always been a guide on a remote island, he had that big town vibe to him. She couldn't quite put her finger on it but he seemed more than what he was portraying himself to be.

"Why don't we take our wine with us and have a walk down the beach, I have something I want you to see."

"Can it wait until the morning?"

"No, you have to go at dusk to get the full effect I really think you will appreciate it, come on it will only take a few minutes and then I will walk you to your hotel."

"Ok, but only for a few minutes I need to get some things ready for tomorrow."

In all fairness, she was completely packed and ready, she was very prepared but she didn't want to create a bond with the man and to tell the truth he made her feel emotions that she had never felt before. It was scary to think that with all the men she had been exposed to none had given the effect Mathew was. Her palms were sweaty, her throat felt dry, scorched almost and her heart was beating like crazy. He had surprised her after they started talking and that rarely happens to Alicia. Every time the breeze blew his scent floated in her direction, it was like breathing in pure masculinity with a side of fresh clean cotton. The beach was so beautiful and being there with him made her completely oblivious to her normal reaction to men. She couldn't allow herself to feel this way, to be exposed and soft. Alicia was so used to keeping herself cut off from emotion that she found herself in an odd spot, even when she had been semi involved, she had never felt like this. It had always been a relationship of convenience, lust or even business. She was very careful not to involve her heart. She tried to keep some space in between them as they walked but something just made her gravitate towards him. Once she almost ran into him, she stumbled and he steadied her, his hands had gripped her waist for only just a few seconds but it felt like a fire burning under her clothes. His touch made her tremble as she played it off to the wine the sand, and the cool breeze coming off the water. She hated the thought of him knowing the way he made her feel. She would become vulnerable in is eyes and she didn't want him try anything, she couldn't trust herself with him, and he was her guide. She couldn't think of him like that, could she?

They walked down the beach in a slow relaxing pace sipping their wine. She had already had enough to drink but she needed to keep her mouth busy, she was afraid that if they were not drinking they would have to carry a stronger conversation and she could barely think straight, although she needed to say something to break the silence. "This is a good bottle; you have good taste in wine." Her voice came out quieter than she had intended but Mathew hadn't seemed to notice, or either he was just being polite.

"Thank you he said I had a little practice as a kid, my parents owned a small vineyard on one of the near by islands and so I was always around it. This is one of ours."

"Really, wow that is amazing. I would love to see it before I have to leave the island, if you wouldn't mind. Is it still producing?" "Yeah we do a little here and there nothing major. Oh, here is the spot; we made it just in time to see them."

"But I don't see anything."

"Just wait in about 2 minutes and, there they are."

"Oh my I have never seen that in all my travels. I have to get this on film do they do this every night?"

"Yeah most nights."

There was a very steep ledge of rock on the far end of the next island but in viewing sight at night with only the moon to cast shadows. The penguins were all atop this cliff gathering together. They were such fascinating animals; they all seemed to jump at the same time over the cliff diving into the dark blue water below. They jumped out of the water in and out as if they were playing and swimming for fun they were actually hunting the krill that migrated to the cliffs edges at night for the warmth of the moons rays.

"Did you know Mathew that the penguins as well as the sea lions, fur seals and most of the other life on these islands came here due to the constantly changing rough currents of the water? Penguins can survive here because of the cold rich waters of the Antarctic Humboldt current that flows around these islands. Most all of the species here was brought by currents, wind or seedlings of vegetation. Charles Darwin was one of the first to research here on the islands in 1835. Oh look, there right outside the realm of penguins. The dolphins are jumping too, there has to be fifty of them, I have never seen a group that big before. This trip is definitely going to prove some theories about these species that we had not known before. Thank you for bringing me here,"

she looked over at him, He was staring at the water and the moon was sparkling diamonds on his thick dark hair. He was so incredibly sexy in the moon light.

"Alicia, he startled her. You seemed lost just then is something wrong?"

"Oh uhh no just thinking about the penguins, can we head back now I'm really exhausted, and I need to get some rest before our long day tomorrow."

"Yeah sure."

They walked back in silence just enjoying the night. She was still thinking about his thick chest with the black curls and his thick arms, "oh stop it you should not be thinking about this guy he is only a guide, and he is much younger by at least five years." Nevertheless, she could not get him out of her mind, she was starting to lose control and Alicia Valamos did not lose control. She tried thinking of something else but her mind always slide back to his beautiful etched body. She was feeling so moist all the way down to her most sacred place and

"Do you want me to walk you in?"

"What?"

"Were her at your hotel did you want me to walk you in?"

"Oh uh no thank but, can you come up in the morning and help me down with my things? My room number is 4230."

"Yeah sure, how about 8:30 and we can catch some breakfast before we shove off."

"Ok thank you I will see you in the morning."

She had to get away from him for the night she needed a cold shower to relax her and take the edge off.

" I really don't know how I'm going to spend so much time with Mathew on that island, alone with him all day"

just thinking about him sent her into shivers and not cold ones. She left him standing in front of the hotel. It was as if she was in a race to get to her room before she started to show her raw need. As soon as she got upstairs to her room, she went into the bathroom slipped out of her clothes and got into the hottest shower she could stand. Stripping off the day in water and suds usually made Alicia feel renewed but tonight it was not as satisfying as it usually was. She stood in the hot spray for an hour and she just could not shake the thoughts of Mathew out of her head. After her unsuccessful shower, she toweled her long hair and braided it for the night hoping to push Mathew out of her mind so that she could get some rest. She turned all the lights down and climbed into the very tall four-poster bed, it felt like climbing into a giant pillow. It was soft with satin sheets at the highest thread count imaginable, she would normally have fallen asleep easily but tonight was different. With all of the memories that had flooded back earlier in the afternoon and now with her erotic thought of her guide that she didn't know at all she could not find her dreams. She lay awake thinking of the memories, trying to figure out why now, Why after all this time would she start to remember things so far in her past that she thought they were gone forever. What triggered these memories and how could she turn them off. She found herself conflicted, she didn't want all those bad memories messing up her tranquility but she did long to remember Katie. What had happened to her, where is she now, is she happy? Her mind was going so fast with bits and pieces of memory laced with pictures of Mathew in her mind that it was going to be impossible to sleep. After about an hour of tossing and turning, she got up, headed for the mini bar, and poured herself a brandy to calm herself. Alicia was not a heavy drinker but tonight she needed a way to get to sleep. She went back to the big bed and crawled in, another half hour and she was finally sleeping.

Katie, Katie where are you honey, where are you. Call out to me Katie let me help you, Katie I can't see you, where are you. I can protect you Katie he won't hurt you anymore, tell me where you are.

Alicia awoke sitting straight up in her bed, panting as if she had just ran a marathon. For a split second, she could not remember where she was. She reached for the bedside table to turn on the lamp

and found her self in the middle of the bed with all
the covers strewn across the room in the floor. She
was sweating and felt like she was having a panic
attack. What was wrong with her, more than likely
just those memories in the park she thought to
herself before crawling off the bed and retrieving
the covers, she had apparently thrown in her sleep.
She found that she had also knocked off the alarm
clock that had been sitting on the bedside table next
to her. She picked it up, it was 3am. She growled at
herself and crawled back into bed. She tried to
remember what she had dreamt to cause such a
scene but could not recall, she slowly drifted back
to sleep this time sleeping until morning.
Mathew stood there outside of the hotel watching
Alicia walk away from him again. Every time she
walked away, it felt like she was intentionally
leaving him. What was it about this girl that set him
off so much? He some how could not get the idea
of her walking away from him out of his mind, he
hated it. Why was this so damn frustrating. He
finally started walking to the docks and went
aboard his boat. He climbed down below and took
off his shoes. He sat on the edge of his bed and put
his head in his hands. What in the world was his
problem, he didn't even know this woman and she
was giving him problems already. He needed to get
this girl out of his head; he did not need this kind of
drama in his life. He was fine being alone, yea he

enjoyed the occasional company of a woman but they knew the score. Mathew finally laid down and found sleep.

Chapter 3

Alicia got up with the alarm at 6am reluctantly. She
sluggishly made her way to the shower to wake up
and got dressed in the sturdy clothes she had
brought with her for her first trip out to the island.
She wore simple cotton panties and bra both white
for comfort, she topped it with a good sturdy pair
of form fitting jeans, a brown leather belt to match
the boots and tank with a cotton t-shirt on top. She
knew it was important to dress in layers when
going on an expedition just in case. She had packed
the jacket and a extra suit of clothes in a back pack
along with her digital camera, binoculars, cell
phone, emergency battery charger, and plenty of
socks jus incase water did penetrate the new boots
she had bought at Gran's and of course her wet
suite. They would be going to Darwin Island first
and then on to Isabella where she would be able to
observe her favorite the penguin, she hoped that
she would get a chance to witness the giant tortoise.
Although her study did not include them she very
much wanted to observe them on her own, she
loved the very idea of them.
She carried a first aid kit and a small survival kit
with her everywhere she went, it was packed in her
back- pack. She twisted her braid up and clipped it;
she didn't want it getting in her way of the camera

lens today on the island. She did not wear any makeup when she was working, she didn't need it anyway she had perfect skin. Just then, she heard a light knock on the door in the front room of her suite. She went to answer and it was Mathew right on time.

"Hey are you ready to go downstairs and get some breakfast before we shove off"

Yeah just, give me a minute to grab my bag.

She went into the bedroom to get her bag. Mathew stood there stunned, of course, she looked good yesterday in her soft pink skirt, but wow did those jeans show off her figure. He hadn't noticed how tiny her waist was and how her hips curved perfectly to accent her backside. He was shifting his legs without notice to accompany the growing bulge in his own jeans. She came back in the room and he quickly turned form her asking to use her bathroom before they left. What is wrong with me, she is a client! Besides, she would never go for a guy like me anyway. He tried to calm himself down in the privacy of her bathroom, finally having control over his body again, he emerged and they went down stairs to eat.

"Here allow me to carry that for you"

Did you pack your wetsuit?

Yes, I have it with me.

Ok well I had all your equipment air lifted to Darwin by helicopter and is waiting there for us except for the smaller shelter; it is onboard just in case something was to happen. Ok let's go then. They went downstairs and Alicia was so caught up in their conversation over equipment she barely noticed them leaving the hotel. "Aren't we going to have breakfast before we go?

 Yeah, unless you have changed your mind?

"No but where are we going I assumed we were eating at the hotel restaurant?

I thought I would take you to my favorite spot; I eat breakfast there almost every morning.

Oh ok that's fine as long as they have coffee!

What's wrong didn't get much sleep last night?

No not too much, I had to do a lot of packing. She didn't want him to know about any of her problems with the memories or the dreams, and definitely not that she had been thinking about him. They walked into this little café across the street from the docks a couple door down from the hotel and found a table. It was a small place, one that seemed only used by the locals. He ordered a full breakfast and she ordered a bagel and coffee. They ate and talked about the trip in such a way that it seemed like they had known each other their whole lives. It was nice until she thought about it and then it scared her a little. It was nice to be able to talk to him without becoming a complete fool like the night before. At least she could talk straight this morning. She was starting to break her own rules and started to wonder why she couldn't have a little fun while she was here. She wanted the fun all right but she was also a little frightened that she would end up with more than she bargained for.

The boat ride to the island was a quiet one, Mathew was navigating the water and Alicia had her camera out taking as many pictures as she could to document the entire trip. While Alicia was taking pictures and recording notes in her book about the scenery and the trip so far Mathew had started watching her out of the corner of his eye. She looked so girlish with her hair twisted up high in her clip and pencil in her mouth while she read over the notes she had been taking. She was so focused and so sexy, he wanted to lean over to her take her into his broad strong arms and take her mouth with his own. She smelled incredible like fresh picked fruit, good enough to eat. Mathew shook his head as if he was trying to let go of the pictures in his mind,

"What am I thinking she is a client and I am just the guide; snap out of it he told himself?"

When they arrived at the Island he anchored the boat and let her know they had arrived, she hadn't noticed because she was so into her notes at that time.

Alicia, were here if you want to go ahead and change into your wetsuit now. The water is very cold so make sure you close it properly. The sharp

protruding rocks around the island made it
impossible to dock the boat at the island. They had
to dock about a half mile out and swim the rest of
the way. This is why Matthew had the bulk of her
equipment flown in earlier this morning.
  Ok thanks where can I change?
*Oh crap what was I thinking, why didn't I wear it
under my clothes*
  Uhh right here?
She made a face at him, she looked around not
even thinking before they left that the boat was
small and didn't really have any privacy. It did
have a small room in the bottom, Mathew called it
his cabin but it was barely big enough to house a
bed smaller than a normal sized twin and just
enough floor space to stand in. It would have been
very hard to change in because there was not
enough room to stand up fully and to get into a
wetsuit was hard enough without being in a tiny
confined space. Besides that, Mathew liked the fact
that she was going to have to change in front of
him so he didn't even offer the cabin.
  She then looked around, as prepared as she always
was she had not thought this decision out
thoroughly. She would have to change into her
wetsuit right here on the boat, in front of him, the
sexy as hell guide. Crap!
You will have to turn around please she said with
as much courage as she could muster, although he

had to have heard her voice crack. He didn't say anything just turned and started undressing himself to get into his wetsuit. As Mathew turned around he felt her eyes on him but tried to pay no attention, if she wanted to look he was definitely going to give her something to look at. He would have kept his boxers on but because she was looking he decided to take them off, it was more comfortable that way! Alicia saw Mathew start stripping and she couldn't bring herself to look away.   As soon as he heard her move he started getting dressed more quickly, maybe he could catch a glance at her without being caught, after all, she did look at him. Why should he be the good one and not look?

 He stripped all the way down taking off everything even his boxers; wow was she staring at him undressing? She covered her eyes and blushed; he had the smoothest skin and tightest ass she had ever seen. She quickly turned all the way around not to be temped to look anymore. She started undressing quickly to hopefully finish before he did so he wouldn't get a look at her. She loved her body and was not ashamed of it but she did not want to give herself any reason to be more attracted to this man, and if he looked at her when she was vulnerable with those deep tantalizing eyes she would just have to jump him right there on the boat.

They finished getting dressed and put on the scuba gear Mathew had packed yesterday. Alicia packed her clothes in her backpack.

Is there always this much fog around the islands in the morning? Darn he had waited too long; he did not even get to see a bare shoulder. Oh well, its better this way he didn't need any more reason to have to hide his man-hood around her, he had already gotten into an embarrassing situation once with his body not cooperating with him today. Mathew looked at her and started laughing, this is not typical no usually there is more, and yesterday was an exception for some reason that is why you were able to see the other island in the moon light. Normally you can't see anything, the fog is usually very dense here and misting constantly. We also have El Niño's with very severe weather, but it looks like we will have an ok day today maybe some storms later on this afternoon so we have to keep an eye out on the weather changes. I will worry about the weather you just do your research, is that a deal?

Ok, she did know how volatile the weather could get in these remote places and that was the only reason for her hesitation when she was told she was coming here. The weather could change in a mater of minutes and she was not looking forward to any of that.

Alicia sat on the edge of the boat dangling her feet
in the cold water on the back end of the boat;
Mathew had already jumped in and was helping
Alicia to put on her water shoes to protect her feet
from the sharp rocks close to the shore. She jumped
in moving her snorkel gear down over her face and
went under the icy water. It was not very easy
maneuvering with the waterproof backpack but she
had to bring her clothes, and lucky for him his fit in
her bag as well, what did he normally do for dry
clothes once on the island? Then she had to stop
herself from thinking, she was imagining him
naked on the island until he caught her attention.
He motioned to her and she moved along with him
in the water. They had decided to use the snorquel
gear so that she might catch a glimpse of some of
the wild life on the way to the island. The view was
amazing; they were not very far from shore but far
enough that she was seeing many different species
of fish with bright colors. They lingered there for a
while allowing Alicia to take pictures of the fish in
their natural habitat with her under-water camera.
Mathew stayed back and watched her as she
enjoyed herself; he was beginning to think that he
saw more in her than just a fabulous body. No that
couldn't be it, it has to be the scenery, Mathew
didn't have relationships he avoided them at all
cost to his sanity, but he could not deny there was
something different about the way he saw Alicia,

she was different some how. She was a real woman
and he admired her focus and ability to ignore him,
he was use to all the women he had known flocking
to him like little puppies offering themselves up
like a snack. He hated that, well he was a man so of
course he took what they offered most of the time
anyway. Alicia had only been on the island a day
and a half but for even that short of a time he can't
remember looking or thinking of another woman.
Oh come on what was wrong with him, he liked the
attention the other girls gave him, he liked that
there was no strings, didn't he? He pushed the
thoughts out of his mind, was he going crazy or
was it her that was pushing him right over the edge
of sanity without her even realizing it?

Chapter 4

When they finally reached the island they took
great care in mounting the Island, the shoreline was
covered in sharp thick volcanic rock. The rock
jutted out in all directions making the accent on
land difficult, Mathew went first turning back to
help Alicia navigate the large rocks to the edge of
the land. It was not at all, what she had expected,
she had read several books on the islands and done
plenty of research but nothing can compare to
seeing it firsthand. The Island itself is not of great
importance to Alicia but the marine life that it
seems to attract. The vegetation was low lying and
was teaming with different species of birds like the
very rare red-footed bobby. She was in augh and
Mathew was exploring around himself, he had been
here a couple of years back but it had been a while.
Being here with her was different than most of his
guided tours that he had done, she was
invigorating; different somehow than when she was
on the mainland. He could tell that this was truly
her passion and he was mesmerized by her
enthusiastic attitude. She was like a little school
girl on her first field trip and he just couldn't get

enough of her smile. It was so real and he loved the fact that she didn't try to hide her emotion.

The trip to the island was a long one and they had lingered in the water longer than he had expected. He wanted to get to the drop location and find her equipment to set up her shelter so that when the heavy rain of night came they would not be caught unprotected.

They made their way to the drop location, which was in the middle of the island to help protect them from high waters if it was to storm; Mathew started unpacking the shelter while Alicia was unpacking her tripod camera and underwater video camera. She was so excited to get an early start tomorrow on the fish around the island and hopefully she could set up her underwater video feed and catch some bigger game. Mathew was drilling holes in the black rock of the island to insert the poles of the temporary structure into the ground. He wanted it to be sturdy; this island sometimes received high winds off the Atlantic. Once all the poles were tightly in the ground he then un- tied the massive canvas that went over the poles to make the shelter. The canvas was a dark earth tone with ridges that helped the water runoff. He spread the canvas along the poles and tied it down in twenty different places along the top and bottom of the poles securing it in place. He then went inside secured the last canvas making the structure into two different rooms and unpacked the cots him and Alicia would be sleeping on for the remainder of the trip. This was their home base but they would use the boat to take day trips to the surrounding islands, and had a smaller enclosure for nights spent on the other islands. As he finished the shelter, Alicia walked in and took a look around the quarters where she would be staying for the remainder of the trip. She silently gasped at the thought of being in the same tent as him at night every night, it scared her because she was on fire just having him near her, and now this was just great she wouldn't be getting any sleep, not with him so close. What she didn't know was that he was there thinking the same thing but they were both so stuck in their ways that neither of them would ever admit they were attracted to each other. Had she not thought of this on the mainland? She knew her shelter only had two rooms and it had never created problems before. She was used to her assistants staying in their own tents, and mostly the institute sent them their individual shelters but She had been so caught up in him that she hadn't even asked if he would have his own shelter, the institute usually sent several tents but I guess because she went alone they had only sent the one. Did they not think of her having a guide?

Oh how wonderful this was gonna be.. She was silently cussing herself for assuming there would be different accommodations for each of them when she was pulled out of her thoughts by him staring at her. She shook the thoughts and threw herself into work conversation with Mathew, that is what she would do she would be all work and no play. That's the only way she could see of keeping her sanity having to be so close to this man. She didn't even share a tent with her fellow co-workers, not even other women she worked with. She didn't like to be that close to anyone. She liked no she needed her own space..

Mathew did you see a generator when you opened the crates that my equipment came in?
Yes, there was a small one but it will only be enough energy to give us light for about 100 hours, they sent very little extra fuel. The sun had started going down, the temperature was dropping and they still had to set up the inside part of the structure. I will set the beds up in that corner over there; it has a flap to divide it so it will be the warmest area. We can put all your equipment in the other side.
"So they were even going to be in the same side together that was just great."
She wanted to ask him why he didn't have his own shelter but she didn't want to sound rude and she

needed a guide she could not be out her alone. How was she ever going to get any rest with him so close and radiating all his male scent around her. He smelled so enticing. She was going to put the blankets in the bedroom part of the tent and he was headed for the equipment side. When they passed, they brushed up against each other and she nearly fell, he caught her with his right arm and pulled her close to steady her on her feet. She looked up at him and they both stood very still for a minute just taking each other's scent in staring in to each other's eyes. He broke contact first and she blushed, said she was sorry, and almost ran into the bedroom. She sat on one of the cots Mathew had just resurrected and put her hands on either side of her head. If she couldn't get through this one night how in the world was she going to get through the rest of this trip and get any work done at all. She wished to herself this was a personal trip and she was with him, well she could dream anyway. She would never have gone for anyone like him before. She didn't want anyone that was capable of falling in love because she could not make that type of commitment to anyone. She made herself get up and finish making both the beds. If this structure was it then she would try to make the best of it and get as much work done as she could and quickly. She feared being with him all alone, she was in

very real danger of doing something she knew she
would regret later when she was back home.
In the other room, Mathew was having his own war
in his mind; He was trying not to think of her that
way. He just hoped that she didn't walk in while he
was in this state, he never had a problem
controlling himself and for some reason this
woman had a hold of his body and wouldn't let go.
He was so hard he knew that he was going to hurt
tonight; there goes his good night sleep. How was
he going to get through this trip if he couldn't even
be in the same room with her without his body
playing tricks on him like this? When he had
touched her arm it was like lava, his hands felt like
they were on fire and it spread from his hands all
they way through his body down to his depths and
rocked his core. This woman was giving him a
fever he could not shake.

Alicia walked through carrying her laptop and said
that the beds were ready, she set the laptop down
on the table that Mathew had unfolded and said that
she wanted to look up some facts about the
different species of fish before she turned in for the
night. He gave her some space and hurried outside
and looked at the sky trying to decide weather or
not it was going to storm tonight, he decided it
might so he tied everything down that wasn't
already. He was giving himself plenty of time to

calm down before he returned into the shelter for the night, maybe if he took long enough she would go to bed and be sleeping when he was done securing everything outside. He had already covered the boat earlier while Alicia had been exploring around the camp looking for birds. He would wait until tomorrow to set up their make shift shower tent. If he were lucky, she wouldn't want a shower that would be hard for him not to take a peak.

Alicia finished up and went to the bedroom taking refuge to change clothes into something warm to sleep in. She had brought a pair of sweats and a long-sleeved cotton shirt so that she was comfortable, glad now that she had decided to pack the bulk of her island gear in the cargo that Mathew had airlifted earlier. It would have been difficult to carry everything from the boat all the way to camp, it had taken them a good hour to hike it earlier. She climbed in and covered herself all the way up to her chin fearing Mathew would come in. She wanted to be asleep before he came in to get ready for bed. She could not bare the embracement of him catching her looking as he changed and she couldn't help herself. I guess she got her wish because she was sound asleep in just a few minutes, Mathew came in to find her quietly breathing and was glad she was sleeping. He got down to his underwear and crawled into his bed, he was out before he knew it.

Katie, Katie where are you honey, where are you. Call out to me Katie let me help you, Katie I can't see you, where are you. I can protect you Katie he won't hurt you anymore, tell me where you are.

Alicia awoke to the same terrified dream as the night before, but this time Mathew sat beside her holding her rubbing the back of his hand across her cheek. She looked up at him with questions in her eyes but did not pull away, she was glad he was there comforting her, she was sweating and breathing very hard just like the night before. He pulled her close to hold her and she did not resist. For what seemed like a long time, he just held her, then after her breathing had settled down he asked her

"are you ok, you were very upset in your dream! Who is Katie?" She tried shifting away and he allowed her to move away from him reluctantly. She stayed close enough that he was still touching her with the skin of his arms; they were so warm it felt like fire on her skin. She sighed and asked if they could talk later, she just wanted to get some sleep. He didn't want to pry so he didn't ask any more questions. He got up and helped her back into her covers and went to lay down in his own bed right across from her and they both went to sleep until morning.

Chapter 5

Mathew woke up the next morning with the break
of dawn, he had to get up he just could not lay there
anymore. He got out of bed, pulled a pair of loose
jeans on and went over to where Alicia lay sleeping
softly. He bent over her and softly brushed a strand
of hair that had come lose from her clip out of her
sweet peaceful face. He looked at her for a few
minutes wondering what could have caused her to
have such a bad dream last night but decided not to
say anything to her about it. If she wanted to
confide in him, he would listen but he didn't want
to push the issue. He felt so close to her, so
protective of her. He knew there was a need for her
protection but he didn't know from what, but he
would find out and he would protect her. What he
couldn't figure out is why he felt so strongly about
it, why was this woman so quickly becoming more
than just a client? As tough as she tried to portray
herself, he knew that she was very much a woman
inside and in need of someone to listen and be there
for her. He had never wanted to be that man for
anyone before but something in him broke last
night when he heard her screaming and crying. He
could not make himself stay away from her, he just

wanted to hold her and let her know that from now on with him she would be safe from whatever demons she had locked away. He was going to get breakfast started and make coffee, giving her some time to rest; she had a long night and needed to sleep it off. He started the coffee, it wasn't long before the bacon, and eggs were sizzling on the small camp propane stove.

Alicia woke up to the wonderful smell of coffee bacon and eggs. She rolled off the cot and sat on the side rubbing her face in her hands, she didn't remember much about her dream last night but she did remember the feel of Mathew's arms around her holding her and the touch of his hand on her face. She felt awkward to go into the next room where he was apparently fixing breakfast for the both of them; she didn't want him to think she was so needy. She was always the one on her expeditions taking care of everyone, and now this tall dark guide was taking care of her even while she slept. How is that going to effect their working relationship or working arrangement she didn't have relationships. She would pretend last night hadn't happened and just go on with the day. She hesitantly got up and went into the front room without even brushing her hair, the food smelled to good to wait she was starving. He was bent over the small camp coking stove retrieving the food from the skillet when he heard her come through the canvas panel that separated the two make shift rooms. She was beautiful in the morning; her hair was wild around her face having come lose from its clip at some point in the night. She was smiling at him with rosy cheeks, and asking about the coffee.

"Here you go one hot steamy cup of coffee would you like sugar or cream?"

Yes, please two sugars and one cream. He was extremely sexy this morning, he wore nothing but an old pair of lose fitting jeans low on his perfect hips so low that she could tell he wasn't wearing anything underneath. His hair hung long, he wore a simple braided leather bracelet on his tan wrist, and his feet were bare. I was staring at the front of his jeans thinking about how good it felt when I woke up in his arms last night and...

"Alicia"   huh what? Oh crap he caught me looking he was smiling the biggest grin I had ever seen. Uh I was day dreaming, thinking… I was thinking umm about cameras my cameras… So how are you with electronics?

I'm ok why, he laughed a little?

Well I want to set up my underwater video feeds today so I can start observing the fish species around the island on the different sides and see if I can catch some footage of the bigger ones like the whale and sharks that are native to these waters. Can you help me; I need extra hands when setting these up under the water? I pretended not to notice as he caught me and went straight into talking about work.

Yeah sure, here is your breakfast I hope you like bacon and eggs. Who doesn't, thank you but you didn't have to cook for me, that's not in your job description ya know.

Yeah well, I'm hungry as soon as my feet hit the ground, and I like to cook.

I'm sorry about that I usually don't sleep late; it's something about the island that has been making me …different.

What do you mean?

Alicia was quiet for a few minutes so Mathew decided to change the subject, she would tell him what was bothering her when she was ready.

So is the plan to stay on the island today setting up underwater cameras? What else do you want to accomplish today, or should I say do you need me for anything except the cameras?

Um no I don't think so why do you have something you need to do?

Well I wanted to set up our shower enclosure today; I know that you're not going to want to smell me after today when the heat gets strong. I thought you might enjoy a shower before bed tonight. Yes said Alicia that would be great, please do take the time out today to complete that lovely task, is there anything else we need to do to complete our set up?

Well I do need to set up the little bathroom tent, Ill
do that after breakfast.
Yes, thank you,
 Oh and Thank you for breakfast it was really good,
I didn't think I would be eating quite this good out
here.
You're welcome.
 Ok well I'm going to go and get dressed for the
day, Ill be out of your way in a few minutes.
When she was in her wet suit, she came out to see
that Mathew was in his as well. The suit fit her
every curve and showed off all her assets. When
Mathew turned to see her pouring a thermos full of
coffee he crossed the small space to her side, he
raised her head with his finger and just looked at
her for a long moment. She just stood there frozen
not knowing what to do; she couldn't will her self
to move away from his gaze and his feathery light
touch on her face. He moved closer, so close she
could feel his sweet breath on her face but he
refrained from touching her body. She wanted in
that moment so badly to step in closer to him to
touch him, to feel the warmth he offered but she
could not move. Her legs felt like Jell-O and she
was lucky she was still standing; it was only by
pure adrenalin that she was still upright. Mathew
knew that when he crossed the room that he wanted
to take her right there. He was just standing there in
front of her, how would she know the battle that

was taking place in his mind as he tried to reason with himself. He knew he should walk out of the tent right now before he made a mistake they would both regret but he couldn't seem to make his feet work. Maybe he could leave if he only knew if she would reject his advances or not. Maybe if he just made a small gesture towards her, she would kick him out screaming, call the entire job off, and find another guide. If she found another guide, she wouldn't be his client anymore and he wouldn't feel so compelled to have only a business relationship with this woman. If... If... oh what the hell, he reached one hand around her waist with the lightest of touch and it felt like molten lava on his skin under her wet suit. She tried to look away from his gaze so he wouldn't see the pure animal lust in her eyes but she could not break the connection. He felt her eyes on him and the heat from her body and it gave him the opening from her he had been hoping for. He pulled her close, so close that she was touching him body to body. He bent his head ever so slightly and brushed his lips across her own so gently she was screaming inside wanting him but she couldn't, could she? He dropped his other hand and wound them both around her waist pulling her even closer where she could feel the full length of his hard body pressing against her. She mustered up enough courage and energy to wrap her arms around his neck as he tilted his head into the nape of her neck and smelled her hair. As soon as she made the little movement, everything changed. Mathew felt the desire in her rush to the surface and he planned to take full advantage of it. He came down on her mouth hard with a fire that she had never before felt in her life, it felt like he had wanted her for years, but she had only know him a couple of days. He took her mouth with his and pushed his tongue far into her full lips, she curled one leg around his thigh to keep her self-upright. This was it she wasn't thinking clearly anymore, he could have her at will. She would give him anything as long as he didn't stop. He slid his hands down her back to grip her butt and lifted her onto his waist and she gladly wrapped her legs around him. He pushed her up against the wall and was kissing her ferociously. She had to have him right now she could feel every nerve in her body pulsating and wanting more. She had never known this type of raw need for another man; he was tearing her insides apart without even knowing it. He carried her to the bedroom and put her feet on the floor, she thought she would fall but somehow pulled enough strength from deep inside to hold her balance. He looked at her with her lips red and swollen from his kisses and started kissing her neck while he undone her wetsuit. He peeled it off her, kneeling in front of her to take it completely off of her. He was bent on his knees in front of her with his hands sliding down her arms to her narrow waist down her curvy hips to her legs. He nudged her to step out of the suit and she obeyed without a word. There she was in front of him with only a bra and panties that covered very little. She never even once thought to cover herself, she wanted him to see her. He was still bent down and slid his hands up her legs to her waist, Alicia's skin felt like baby's skin. She was soft creamy and undeniably beautiful. He gently slid the thin lace panties off her small waist with a little grunt from her

" I want to see all of you"

She wanted him to see her she just could not hold her excitement in but said nothing, only obeyed his request. She stepped out of them and he looked over her with his all-seeing eyes. She felt safe and alive in so many ways, Mathew made her feel safe and crazy all at the same time. He stood slowly taking her all in and then un-hooked her bra and she was all his to look at. She was so beautiful. He took her mouth again this time it was soft and sensual, he could feel the tension in her body and wanted to ease it. He wanted to take her hot and fast but he wanted her to trust him, to know he would take care of her to know that he cared? Did he really care about her, yes he did he really did care about her and wanted to keep her safe in his arms. Something about Alicia brought out the protective side of Mathew, but what did she need protection from? He slowly trailed a line with his fingertips down her body to her center; she was hot and steamy for him. She felt his hand cover her most intimate of places and she could barely breathe. Mathew noticed immediately that she was smooth at her core, he loved that she took such good care of her body.

Something was so sexy about her being completely naked in front of him. So erotic yet so different from anything she had ever felt. She wanted to tell him right then that she was falling for him but how could she, oh, there were his hands again, she could not think right now. That is what it was, not love she just could not think with his expert touch on her. He gently laid her on the cot and stood to take his wetsuit off. He pooled it in the floor at his feet, to her excitement he was wearing nothing underneath. She looked at his broad tight chest and followed the trail of curls all the way down his flat rippled stomach all the way to his rock hard shaft that was standing so tall that she felt a little intimidated. Her body went crazy with excitement and in that moment, she needed him inside her. He gently laid on the small cot beside her his shaft up against her flat stomach. He started kissing her again on her neck nipping her with his teeth cupping her full breast with his big hands. Taking things slowly making sure she wouldn't regret this

tomorrow, he wanted this to be as special for her as it was for him. He never took his time, he always just got what he wanted while giving the girl, what she wanted and it was over. For some reason he didn't want this to end, he wanted to keep her all to himself. He slid his mouth down her neck and settled on her bright pink peaks and flicked them with his tongue making them hard and her breathe caught. She arched her back trying to get closer to him, but he wanted to please her in every way.
" I want to taste you" She almost lost control, he eased himself down the length of her pressing light tantalizing kisses all the way down her body until he found his target. She let her hips and legs fall open to accommodate his large upper body, he grabbed her hips in his hands and just looked at her. She was amazing; she had big full lips that were the perfect color of pink and olive. She was shaved completely allowing him to see all of her most private of places. She could feel his breath on her and tried lifting her hips to meet him, he took in the smell of her warmth, and it was like jasmine. He touched her with his mouth and she jumped, he looked up at her, smiled, and went back to her center to pleasure her at his will. Mathew licked her moist center as she raised her hips to him and then without warning he plunged his tongue deep into her moist pink folds. Her sheath was so hot and moist he loved the taste of her, he nipped at her and

that sent her spiraling out of control. Alicia could not seem to raise her hips high enough to him, she wanted so much more from him, He was making her pulse race and her skin was hot. How could this happen she wanted to scream but heard no sound only in her mind, she softly cried out as he took her to new levels of pleasure she had never experienced before. She had her hands wrapped tightly in his long hair lifting her legs to allow him better excess to her. She could not stand it any more her body rippled with pleasure and pulsed under the strokes of his tongue, He drank her in and raised his body over hers. She begged him for more although she didn't think she could possibly get any higher than she had just been. He was so hard he could not resist her he had to be inside of her. He settled himself between her thighs and pushed his thick head into her folds, she was so tight he slammed into her. Over and over again, he filled her with his body, in and out fast and hard he took her all of her for his own. He felt Alicia tighten around him and knew he had taken her over that edge again. He pulled away from her with her hands reaching for him she had not had enough yet. He turned her around on her hands and knees and plunged into her again holding her hips. He pulled her hips to him shoving himself deep inside the tight folds of her center. He let go in one big push and his hot cock filled her cavity with streams of himself. She could feel him get harder and then let go. He slowed and remained inside her as he pulled her hair to the side to kiss the creamy skin on the back of her neck.

Chapter 6

Laying beside her now both of them in silence he held her in his arms and she nuzzled deep into his chest feeling safe and loved. *"He cant love me I know that so why does it feel that way?"* she asked herself. She let the thought go and just enjoyed being in his arms, she loved the smell of him and being wrapped up in his arms was the safest place she had ever known. He was running one hand up and down the small of her back absentmindedly. She was so soft and fit perfectly into his arms he didn't understand how this happened, she was perfect they were perfect, now he just had to convince her of that fact. He had a feeling that was not going to be an easy thing to do, it had not just been sex to him but somehow he felt it was to her. He didn't know how or when but he was already falling in love with her and there she was in his arms naked against his body, he immediately was hard again. She looked up and read his mind this time it was slow and tender and when they had finished half the day was gone. When they did get up and leave the bed, she didn't feel embarrassed like she thought she would have she just felt complete for the first time in her life, but what was he feeling? There was no awkwardness between them just affection, is was as if they had been together for years. Mathew got dressed and told her he would help her install her underwater video cameras so that she could start her research. He thought to himself how he was going to convince her that she loved him too, well he had plenty of time, he would take things slow make sure he took up much of her time with love making so that her research would take longer to complete. Maybe she would decide to stay with him

" *Mathew lets not get ahead of our self she might not like you at all, no not with the passion they shared*" Ha ha " *I bet this island has never seen our kind of passion*"

What are you laughing about, Alicia was standing there staring at him.

"Oh nothing just thinking, so are you ready to get those cameras in the water?"

"Yeah sure, I have everything ready."

They got dressed in their wetsuits for the second time of the day and gathered all the gear they would need to set up the cameras. "How many cameras are we going to set up?"

"Well I want to set up cameras at all different points around the island to get as many different angles and species as I can. I thought about putting two cameras on all sides east, west, north ,and

south. I want one up close to the island and one a
little further out to catch the bigger specimens.
Once we get the cameras set, we will be able to run
the feeds to my laptop and get real time pictures
and video so that I know what is out there and how
I need to proceed with my research."
" Will the coldness of the water affect the cameras
durability, or their productiveness?"
"No it should not harm them at all, the institute
sends us out with only the best equipment, besides I
research every locations environment before
deciding what to bring."
 These cameras should have no problems in getting
me the footage I need. They are also almost
invisible down under the water. They were painted
specifically for this trip. It helps me to get better
footage of the species in their own environment
without outside influences. If they see the cameras,
they might act different out of curiosity or fear of
the unknown, so it's very important they blend in
the background. We need to select each cameras
location with care so that they are as un-seen as
possible. Once they are all installed,
I will need a couple of weeks to watch and analyze
the footage before going in to get pictures by
diving. I want to see what changes in behavior they
have with me in the water and without. I can get
my tree seat setup in the mean time and get some
pictures of the species on land. I will see if their

mating habits change because of a foreign person is in their environment.

" ok well we better get started because we only have a few hours of daylight left and we don't want to be in the water after dark not with these wetsuits. We will need thicker ones for that."

After the cameras were set, the sun was fading and it was time for dinner, they had been occupied at lunch and so they were both starving. They went back to camp and Alicia fixed them some dinner while Mathew fixed the shower. By the time, dinner was ready and on the small folding table the sun had set and it was getting much cooler outside. Alicia called to Mathew and they sat down to dinner, they ate in silence at first. Alicia sat there eating slowly thinking about Katie as if she had been ever since they had first got into the water this afternoon putting the cameras into place. She really wanted to tell Matthew about her but didn't know where to begin or if he would even want to know. It was hard for Alicia to think let alone talk about her past, and she didn't even remember all of it. Only bits, pieces, and not a lot of it made since to her how would she explain things to him that she herself didn't understand. Well I guess I have to start somewhere.

"Katie" Alicia said it like a statement.

…. Mathew looked up surprised that she had decided to tell him about her dream, or at least he hopped that was the story he was fixing to get. He sat silent and just watched Alicia, she seemed to struggle to get the words out.

"Katie... was kind of my sister, not by blood or anything but we grew up together for awhile. My parents died when I was very young and since we didn't have any family I went into the foster care system. At that time in London, it was not strictly regulated as if it is now. I was put into this home when I was around seven and my foster parents were; well let's just say they should have never been foster parents. I was there for a couple of years before it started and I haven't thought about it until just recently. I actually put it out of my mind somehow, I guess it was a self-preservation type thing. Something about the islands are making me remember, well dream anyway. I have been trying to put the clips in my dreams together but they are all so distorted. I keep having thoughts about Katie; she was another child in the system that I got very close to. A couple of years after I was put into this particular house, she was placed there too. We quickly became close I guess mostly out of need, we tried to protect each other but I just can't remember from what. I remember feeling anxious and scared as well as very protective of Katie, I guess because she was so much smaller than me. I don't understand how all these years I never thought of it or about her and then all of a sudden I come to the islands and I start dreaming about her. Mathew had just listened to her story trying not to interrupt or push her into telling him more than she wanted to, but he had to know.

"What did you dream?"

"Well I am not really sure all I can remember is being in a cold dark place, I cant tell if it's a house or what but it is an inside structure of some kind. I was in the dark and I was calling out to Katie, I thought she was in trouble somehow, but I don't know from what or who. I remember feeling very scared for her and very mad at myself for some reason. I want to remember but it has been blocked out of my mind somehow and for so long, but I need to find her Mathew. I don't know why or even where to start looking all I know is her name is Katie Johns, and I'm assuming that is her real name. I know that this sounds crazy and that you probably think I'm a nut case but I feel like I'm having these dreams because she really is in some kind of trouble and I need to help her. I just can't seem to shake the feeling that somehow her problems are linked to me and our history growing up some how. I just wish that I could remember more details about our childhood. There has got to be someway for me to find out what happened to her."

" Don't worry we will do some research and we will find her, I will help you."

I'm sorry this is not your burden; I should not be putting this on you... You don't... Mathew cut her off mid sentence, don't go there Alicia I said I would help you and I will. Have you ever been to the islands before, maybe that's what's triggering the memories?

I don't think I have ever been here before, if I had I don't remember it.

Therefore, Mathew said tell me more about when Katie came to live there with you...any little detail could help in piecing this puzzle together. Sometimes it just takes someone else to see the picture more clearly. Alicia started out slow well, she was four and I was eight when she first came to the house.. I remember that she had bruises on her arms and legs and she wouldn't talk. She must have been abused physically somehow. I remember trying to talk to her; I would sneak food up to our room after our foster parents went to bed. They didn't feed us very well and she couldn't get stuff for herself because she was so little. She was four but I remember thinking she was so small she looked like she was two or three. She was always sitting holding her skinny arms around her legs with them pulled up to her chest rocking back and forth. After she was there a while I do remember reading to her and she started opening up to me, she would talk to me and she even crawled into bed with me one night and slept with me every night after that. She had terrible dreams, she would wake up screaming and I would put my hand over her mouth so she wouldn't wake them up, they were mean and would have given her lashes for that. Sometimes she just shook in the dreams and I held her until she calmed down. This went on for a couple of years and she was really comfortable with me, she didn't like it when I went to school but as soon as she had turned five and could go to school, too she seemed better. She was like a daughter or a little sister to me, she depended on me for everything, and I didn't mind. I think it gave me companionship and it took away the lonely hours. We tried to keep to ourself as much as possible when we had to be in the house. We stayed outside all hours of the day until nightfall when we were not in school. We pretended that we were princesses living in a far away land and we had a big castle that had many special secret passages that only we knew about. It was ok for a while we didn't see much of our foster parents and they didn't mind, they just wanted us for the money they received from the government. I remember that when I turned 10 Katie was scared all the time … I can't remember why, but something changed. Before that, we were somewhat happy, as happy as we could be in that type of situation. I keep trying to remember what could have changed to make everything so different but I just can't seem to pull that memory from the past. I don't understand why some things I can see just as if I was back there but then I go blank, Mathew why can't I remember?

Mathew got up and put his plate away, he came to her side of the small folding table and drew her up from her chair and just held her, he didn't know how to help her and she seemed so desperate to find the answers.

He whispered to her, Alicia we will find a way to get to the truth, I will be here for you all the way. Alicia moved away far enough to look him in the face still holding on to him, why are you being so nice to me?

A few minutes of silence passed, Mathew about this morning… I uh … Mathew put his finger over her mouth, don't Alicia this morning was what it was and I don't want you to feel like you owe me anything. I hope you don't regret it…

Mathew I don't regret it… I just don't I mean I don't have relationships. I don't want you to get the wrong idea about us, I'm not capable of giving anyone myself, and …

Alicia, we had some fun, and I want that to last but I'm not offering to marry you or anything! At least not yet…he had a devilish crooked grin on his face. Alicia blushed, I'm sorry I am reading more into this than there is. I will shut up now.

Mathew pulled her close and held her, how could I tell her I'm falling in love with her when she doesn't feel the same and I know it. I will just have to convince her she loves me; I will just have to spend as much time with her as possible until she falls in love with me. Alicia was trying to think but it was hard when she could feel him so close, He made her heart race every time he was in the same room. How could she tell him she was falling for him when he had just said that he just wanted to have some fun? Wasn't that what she wanted? What she had always wanted.. Fun with no strings attached. That was good she liked his kind of fun but the truth was for the first time in her life she wanted more, she wanted him all of him and she didn't want to share him with anyone ever. Was she falling in love with him after one afternoon? How could this possibly be happening to me?

He broke the contact between them and offered her to accompany him outside. She fallowed Mathew still holding her fingers lightly. They walked just outside the tent to the back and she saw the shower, wow that looks bigger than I remember it being. Well your company was generous enough to provide some extra canvas so I improvised a little and made it bigger, we will also have as much hot water as we want, with the bigger generator I found on the cargo plane and the ocean waters being so

close we will have good water pressure and temperature control. How does a shower sound?
 Oh it sounds perfect, do you mind if I go first?
 Mathew just smiled at her, sure that's fine with me. Alicia went inside and got her toiletry bag that held her shampoo, soap, and towel. She went back outside and jumped right in. Once in the shower tent she undressed and was ready to turn on the water, oh no how did she turn it on. With Mathew's alterations, she didn't know how it worked. Crap! She had to ask him, how embarrassing was that?
 Umm Mathew she called… he answered her "yeah."
How do you turn the shower on?
He laughed just a second and Ill show you.
 Ok thanks.
Ugh…. oh did he just say show me… Next thing she knew Mathew was coming into the shower with her completely naked. She looked stunned and he smiled and said I was hoping you would ask me to join you, which is why I made it big enough for us both to fit. She stuttered a little I didn't exactly ask you to join me I just asked "shhh" Mathew turned on the water and it felt so good she stopped complaining and just stood there enjoying the hot wet water. Mathew stood back for a minute letting her enjoy the hot spray and just watched. There was something about taking a shower with her that was almost more intimate than sex. He loved her, he

had known from almost the moment they had met. He moved up close to her, she had her eyes closed and the water was running down her flawless body. He shifted his weight from one foot to the other then pressed his body next to hers as she was facing him, he was so aroused his heat pressed softly into her flat stomach and she opened her eyes. He turned her around, she was expecting him to enter her but he did nothing. He held her then reached for her shampoo bottle and squeezed out too much in his hands she noticed but she said nothing. She was surprised when he started messaging the shampoo in her hair and not his own. He washed her hair messaging the jasmine liquid into her scalp and then in the tendrils laying down her back. He turned her around and gently rinsed the shampoo out in the hot water, it was almost too hot but not as hot as she felt inside with him naked, so close and touching her. He retrieved her body wash from her bag and put it in the palm of his hand, he didn't want to use a cloth he wanted to feel every inch of her while he washed her body clean. He ran his hands over her back then her arms and shoulders. He went to her breast next and lingered feeling the taught nipples react to his touch. He moved down to her waist and reached around to her backside. He lifted her legs one by one spreading the creamy soap up and down each one, and then he found her center. She gasped when he washed her most private places. He loved to be so intimate with her, it was exhilarating. After lingering there too long, he turned her around and rinsed her off one body part at a time. She was so relaxed; she couldn't believe how open she was with this man. She reached for the body wash and intended to return the favor, she needed to touch him. She messaged the soap all over his tight body his neck first, with all his features his neck was the one thing that took her breath away from her lungs. She loved to nuzzle him there; it had kind of turned out to be her safe place in the last couple of days. He made her feel safe and comfortable, something she hadn't felt in a very long time. She made her way down to his thick shaft and for the first time wrapped her fingers around him, Mathew drew in a deep breath at the feel of her touching him. She slid up and down his hard shaft and cupped his balls, they were hanging loosely. She loved the way he seemed to move to her touch, she liked the feeling that she moved him. She liked knowing that his body responded to the feel of her touch and in that moment could not imagine him being touched by any one but her, He was hers and hers alone. She turned him to rinse off the soap because that would burn and she had to have him right now, her body ached for him to the core of her being. She grabbed him and as much as he wanted her, he caught her hands, wrapped them around his neck, and held her there for just a few seconds. He reached around, turned the water off, and got her towel for her.

She was so beautiful in the moon light looking up at him.

She looked at him confused but he wanted her to know that they could be intimate and close without the sex; he wanted her to trust him, to trust in each other. He wanted her trust so she could learn to love him. He wrapped her up in her towel, took his, and ushered her out into the open air.

"Thank you for the shower" he told her

She looked amazing in the moon light, how am I ever going to convince her just how much she moves me? Alicia is all the woman I never thought that I wanted in life. How is it that Alicia just happened to come into my life, and without any warning at all she means more to me in the few days I have know her than anyone has ever meant to me. I have to take my time with her and make sure that she understands just how much I care and hopefully she feels the same for me. It would be easier if she could read my mind and heart some how.

I say we take a shower like that one every day. He kissed her softly, brushing his lips against hers and went inside the tent to get dressed.

Chapter 7

Alicia went inside the tent to find Mathew
dressed in just a pair of boxer shorts, he was
apparently waiting for her, and she had been
standing out in the breeze after her shower drying
out her hair. It was down around her shoulders and
cradling her face. She went into the bedroom to get
her pj's only to find Mathew had pushed their cots
together as close as they would go. She sat down
and they didn't budge, she was a bit curious so she
looked further and he had bound them together
with wire. She sat smiling to herself as she shifted
through her bag for something comfortable to wear
when she thought… she could play this game too.
She would wear nothing but a t- shirt that would
not quite hide her bottom when she stood up and
wear absolutely nothing under it. Now, when he
tries something tonight I will not consent, she was
not mad but a little hurt that Mathew had made her
so excited earlier and then just like that he turned it
off. How could he do that? She had pretended the
need to stay outside to dry her hair but really she
was trying to calm down after being so aroused. He
couldn't really be attracted to her if he could just
turn it off and on like a light bulb, could he? Well
she was about to find out because she was going to
be the one to do the seducing tonight.

He turned around to find Alicia standing right in front of him and heading out the door, was she trying to kill him? She had nothing on but a t-shirt, a very thin t-shirt and it wasn't even long enough to hide her curvy backside. She was biting her plush bottom lip and had a devilish little grin on her face. He hadn't seen that face before but he loved it, he loved getting to know her and all her little faces that he had come to adore. What was he thinking how was he going to prove to her he didn't want just sex when she came out looking like that. He turned away from her so that she wouldn't see the bulge in his boxers grow. After he calmed his self he fallowed her outside walked up behind her brushed the hair off her shoulder, wrapped his arms around her and laid his chin on her shoulder. It's beautiful here isn't it?

As many times, as I have been here I never get over the sight of this place, although it is much better with you here and much more beautiful. From now on to me… this will be our island.

I love you, he so desperately wanted to tell her those three simple little words that meant so much but he didn't want to scare her off so he just stood there with his arms wrapped around her middle and said nothing. Oh how he loved the feel of her next to him, it made him feel alive and excited. His body reacted to hers in a way that set her apart from any other woman he had ever met. She knew that there would be no other to touch him the way Alicia did emotionally or physically. He shuttered at the realization that someone else had touched her before him, He couldn't stand to think of it and he would do everything in his power to make sure that no one but him touched her ever again. She was his and his alone. He wanted her all to himself and some how some way he would make it a reality.

She said nothing. She just turned around and put her arms around his neck lifting her already short shirt even higher revealing almost everything. He cringed and wrapped his hands around her waist wanting to grab her so much but he keeps his composure somehow. She let go and sauntered into the tent laughing. Her laughter was contagious; it was nice to hear it. He stuck his head into the tent and asked her if she would like to come out and sit by a fire. He had collected some twigs and a couple of good logs he had found yesterday while setting up the shelter. She came out and he had her chair sat close to his, he started the fire and told her to watch. When the fire grew big, it was so beautiful he had gotten a log that had been at some point in the salt water so the fire burned in pretty colors. They sat in silence for a while just enjoying the cool night air with the fire burning. They were sitting close enough to hold hands both seemed very content. Alicia got up, moved over to Mathew, and sat in his lap nuzzling her face into the crease of his neck. She loved the smell of him the sheer masculinity mixed with his own male scent, she felt so safe, and she was so tired that she fell quickly asleep with the drum of his heart as a lullaby and her hands in the tight curls of hair in the middle of his chest. Mathew sat still holding her listening to her even breathing, every time she took a breath and exhaled it nearly killed him. Something about the way her breath felt against his neck made him crazy. He got up with her in his arms and walked into the tent, he sat on the edge of the bed that he had made and she woke up.

I hate to wake you honey, but I need to barrow your laptop, is that ok? She just looked up at him…

Alicia is it ok?

Oh, I'm sorry yes, whatever you need.

What were you thinking about just now?

Don't laugh at me but I liked the way you called me honey.

Mathew just laughed.

Alicia tried to get up and Mathew held her tighter, you can't get up without giving me a kiss first. She smiled and touched his lips slowly and softly with her own, then got up and gave the laptop to him. It was a good thing she had internet service out here, he went to work. First, he looked up

"Katie John's"

in the national database. He entered in London England and then the date she would have been born or close. He came up with several and then turned to Alicia who was looking at her underwater camera monitor. Alicia, what color hair did Katie have? She spoke without thinking, it was blonde and her eyes were blue. Good that will narrow this down. Then she turned to Mathew what are you doing? I told you I would help find her, so I'm looking. Any descriptions you can give me will help narrow the search. Do you know her parents names or why she was taken from them or when? No, I'm sorry I don't remember.

Well when we go to the main land for supplies we will go to the local library and do some research, your good at that right, I mean that is what you do. Mathew just thought of it, Alicia you have made your living doing research have you looked for Katie before? No, I haven't. Why, I mean if you were that good why would you have not looked for her before? I hadn't thought about Katie in a long time, I know its sounds crazy but I kind of blocked that part of my life out. I hadn't thought about it until I got here to the islands. What I can't figure out is why being here is bringing back these memories, I am sure I have never been here before, but then again I don't remember a lot about my childhood. You have lived here all your life right Mathew?

Well most of it anyway, I was in the states for a while about 5 years.

Why did you go to the states?

Well I was tired of just being someone's son, here my parents were somewhat famous for the winery and I was always just the son of Edward Black. I wanted to create my own identity, so I moved to the states after going to school and got a job as a homicide detective in New York. I hated it there, I was my own person all right but I missed the tranquility of the islands. You can't breathe in a place like New York. I had already made up my mind to come home to the islands, but I was going to finish out the year then give my resignation. I was called in the middle of that year from Gran and she told me that my parents had been in a car wreck and was gone. I came home to lay them to rest and have been here ever since. I couldn't leave, my parents loved their vineyard and were so proud of it that I had to stay and keep it going so I moved back and there you go. You know I do still have a couple of friends back in New York that I might be able to call in a couple of favors from. Maybe they could put Katie's name through the databases they have and give us something to go on. They have more access than I do. I can still get into some things but I don't know if it will be enough to get a hold of child protective records and the information we will need to find Katie. What were your foster parent's names?

Alicia sat very quiet and then said Beta and Jack Collins. Will that help you to find information on Katie?

Well I can try to locate her by starting where we know she was and going backwards to her parents, and getting as much information on her as possible, Katie may have a different last name or maybe her name is not Katie at all.

How are we ever going to find her if we are not even sure of her real name? I feel like she's in trouble and I can't get to her to help her. Alicia was tensed now and Mathew could see it all over her face, Alicia why don't we get some rest and we will talk more tomorrow. Alicia agreed and she went into the bedroom and laid down in the now big bed, she covered up and thought that maybe trying to seduce Mathew tonight was a bad idea. She only had a thin shirt on and she was cold. Mathew stayed on the computer for a few minutes after Alicia had went to bed and used the time away from her to email a friend.

Hey, how's it going, I haven't heard from you in a while how's the big apple? Hey, man, I need a favor from you; I need to locate a girl that grew up in England that was in foster care. All I really know is that her name is Katie Johns. She was in

the same house as a girl named Alicia Valamos;
the foster parents names are Beta and Jack Collins,
I need to know as much about the both of them that
you can find. I really appreciate anything you can
get. Thanks Man,   oh yeah send the info to my
phone; I don't want anyone to know I'm looking.
Thanks,   M.B

Mathew sent the email and then turned the laptop off and went in to find Alicia curled up in their bed; there was something very comforting about that phrase "their bed" He lifted the covers easily and slid in carefully trying not to wake her. He laid down beside her wrapping her in his arms and she snuggled into them in her sleep. He could feel her naked bottom pressed against him and it took all the strength he had not to wake her up. He laid there thinking of her and her childhood, wanting to know what was eating at her and what it had to do with these islands, his islands. He drifted off with her in his arms and they slept peacefully… together.

Chapter 8

She woke up scooting even closer into his warm
embrace; she almost forgot where she was or why
she was there. She was so comfortable in his strong
arms she didn't want to get up but she thought it
was getting late and their was so much to be done.
What time is it she thought? She carefully slid out
from under his grip trying not to wake him, went
into the other room, and looked at the computer to
see the time. She realized it was late; she had slept
for a long time and noticed she didn't wake up with
nightmares last night like the nights before. She
had dreamt of her childhood, she was sitting on the
front porch of the poor house of her foster parents
and a black car stopped In front. A woman of short
statue got out and with her a tiny little girl with
blonde hair. She took note that it was around Easter
because that is why she was out side she had been
watching the other kids in the neighborhood hunt
eggs. She had wished she were doing the same.
That would mean she knew when Katie came to
live with them, it was April in 1972. She was
remembering more and more, she had a small
raggedy doll with her and it was torn. The lady told
Katie to sit down with me while she went inside to
talk to the foster parents about grown up stuff. The
little girl was very quiet and said nothing; she sat

down away from me on the next step of the porch
where the old paint was peeling off the wooden
post holding it up. The house was relatively small
but did have a good-sized front porch and a second
story. All the rooms were off one hallway or
another, each room separated by a door that
creaked when you moved it. The house did not
have much open space and it was very dimly lit.
Her room was upstairs, it was small with two small
beds maybe toddler beds. They were not quite as
big as twins were and the mattresses were worn and
didn't smell too good. There was one small
window that led into an alley but when she looked
out, she could still see the stars and feel a breeze
sometimes. The window was cracked and it didn't
fir into the window seal perfectly so it let in fresh
air when it was windy outside. She often brought
home pictures she drew at school and put them on
the wall with tape she barrowed from school. It
made it seem more like a real home with something
on the paint peeled walls of her room. They did
have a small basement but she wasn't allowed
down there and didn't want to go anyway. All the
walls needed new paint, the kitchen was small, and
on the back of the house with a door leading
outside into a grown up yard that was in need of a
lawn mower and some trash bags. You could tell by
looking at the house from the outside that the
occupants did little upkeep and that they just didn't

seem to care of the shape the house was in. The house itself almost seemed sad. It was located in the old part of town where all the houses were old and in need to repair. I think in several years past it was more than likely an up and coming neighborhood, it had a school just a couple blocks down and although it was in need of repair too, it looked as thought it had one day been a really nice school. At least the teachers were nice and the food was hot, and it was better than being in that house.

A few minutes later the lady came out of the house got back into the big car and left the little girl without saying a word. We sat on the porch in silence for what seemed like a long time. I wish I could remember more of that dream, it hadn't been so bad like the others. I wanted to tell Mathew before I forgot so I went into the bedroom and sat beside his warm body. I laid my hand on his stomach and he opened his eyes. I'm sorry to wake you but I had a dream, he sat up fast "are you ok"

Yes, it was actually interesting, I know when Katie came to live with me. It was in April of 1972, does that help?

Yes, but how do you know?

I had a dream, I remember her coming during Easter, and I was seven.

Ok that's good we will have a little more to go on just let me email my buddy the info and maybe that will lead us in the right direction, there could not have been that many different girls between that age and date to be placed in foster care. Mathew turned in the bed, come here lay down with me. Mathew I have to get some work done, I have hardly accomplished anything since we got here. Just for a minute, please. Alicia laid next to him and he pulled her on top of him. I just want to hold you Alicia. She straddled him with her nakedness and laid down on his chest with his arms tightly around her. She nuzzled into his neck and was happy. She was actually happy, had she never felt this before? If she had, she couldn't remember when. She was beginning to think she trusted him, how that was even possible she hadn't trusted a man or anybody for that matter since her parents had died, well with the exception of Katie. She had trusted Katie, although she had not felt that until just now. Mathew held her tight, felt her warmth through his boxer shorts, and knew he had better move or he would be all over her. It was as if she read his mind because she sat up still straddling him, she could feel him rising and wanting nothing more than to have him but knew she would get no work done that way. She would end up in bed with him all day and accomplish nothing. She leaned down, brushed the lightest of kisses on his mouth, and got up. He just laid there shocked, she had not started any contact with him and she just kissed him! He didn't make a big deal of it; he wanted her to feel comfortable and relaxed with him. He got up stretching and she was laughing.

"What"

he asked sleepily? Um you might want to adjust yourself some she said giggling, and turned away. He looked down, saw that he was still excited to see her, and was out of the front of his boxers. He got his clothes and asked her if she wanted to take a shower with him, she shrugged and said only if you allow me to take one and get out, I have to get some work done today. I need to go over all the footage from the underwater cameras and see if I caught a glimpse of anything special. I also need to spend some time in the trees today taking pictures of the birds here. What do you have planned to do today?

Mathew looked her up and down and said, to watch you do what ever you have planned today.

She laughed no really?

Well, I need to go back to the boat ant get some supplies and while I'm there do some small maintenance. What do you say we meet back here for lunch?

Alicia smiled and said ok, that sounds nice I will fix us something. Your not against me fishing here are you nature girl?

What, no but try not to disturb the waters where my cameras are please. Ok then I will also be getting dinner for tonight.

Oh yeah, well we will just see how good a fisherman you are and she poked at him.

He laughed and went to take a shower so she went in the other room to grab clothes and she followed him. They took a shower together without anything happening and got busy with their tasks for the day. Mathew put his wetsuit on and headed out into the water to the boat. He wanted to reset the anchor, the water here moved so swiftly with the currents that he didn't want the anchor to lose its ground. He made his way back across the Island to the boat and swan out to it. He mounted the boat and noticed that the cover he had put on it the other day had been moved a bit. He didn't think anything about it; the wind had been a little strong the other night. He started rolling back the canvas and inspected the boat and it seemed fine. He went to the back and reeled in the anchor about half way and repositioned it then dropped it back down into the water getting a stronger hold. The boat had moved some he had noticed but not enough to worry about. He made his way down to the small holding area and packed some food and supplies into a small floating device he used to get the supplies to and from the island with ease. Had he put the flares down here, he always kept a flare gun and plenty of flares on the boat just incase something happened. He could have sworn he put them here, but he couldn't find them. Oh well, maybe he was losing his mind. His pistol wasn't there either, he probly forgot to get that box. When he had first met Alicia on the main island he had spent to much time thinking about her so maybe he had just forgotten to pick up those two things. In all his trips to the islands, he had never had the need to use it before but he liked the idea of being prepared just in case anything was to come up. He was lucky he always had his 9mm on the boat in a safe place, he went and retrieved it from under the built in cooler. It was the perfect hiding place for his gun, he had the boat customized with the secret compartment years ago when he had come back to the islands from New York. He wanted to have his gun with him just in case he needed it for anything. After being a detective in New York, you learn to be prepared for the unexpected. You never know what will come up on you on these islands. Although Alicia was here researching complacent animals, it didn't mean that there weren't any vicious ones here. Alicia had been on his mind, she was dangerous to him. When she was around he forgot all reason, it was good to have a little time to his self so that he could actually think straight. He had to make sure that he kept her safe from any kind of harm, he would not be able to stand it if she got hurt and he wasn't there to protect her. After he packed everything he thought they would need he looked in the back and got a bottle of wine. He always kept it on his boat in case he wanted to relax, and the way she was keeping him wound up all the time he definitely needed something to help him relax. He wondered about Katie and if his buddy from New York had found anything yet, he had emailed him the new information before he come out here and wanted some answers. He knew that was part of the reason Alicia was so closed off from getting close to anyone, he wanted to know why. How were Katie and her foster parents linked to Alicia's self-preserving issues? He wanted to find Katie and unlock the rest of Alicia's past, he wanted to know her and wanted her to be able to let go of the past so that she could finally have a real relationship, and he wanted it to be with him. As far as he was concerned she was already his, he just had to convince her of that fact. The more time he spent with her the more he wanted to be bound to her. Was he sure he was ready for a lasting commitment to a woman that was committed to her work so much that he might actually have to move away from the islands to be with her? That would be a hard decision to make, but he would leave that for another day, right now, he had to concentrate on how to unlock her past and make her trust him. While Mathew was deep into his thoughts, he heard a loud noise and immediately jumped and went topside to see what it was. His heart almost sank to the bottom of the boat, he saw Alicia in the water screaming to him, he dove in after her. When he reached her, he saw that her feet were bleeding and she had scrapes all down her legs and arms, from the volcanic rock around the edge of the water. She was shivering, why wasn't she in her suit? By the time he had made it to her, she was so cold that she had stopped screaming and was sinking in the cold water. He lifted her to the boat and blew air into her mouth, she was blue from the cold of the water. She chocked and opened her eyes. Why did you get into the water without your suit Alicia? Her eyes were big and red from the water. Mathew the cameras… the footage I was going over it and I saw a man. There was a man under the water, he had a gun, he looked right into the camera, and then it went black. I was in the tent so I had my shoes off, I heard a loud noise and so I went outside. There was a man running from the side of the tent back into the trees, I thought their was no one on this island but us. I was so scared that it was the same man I took off running to find you, I wouldn't have went into the water without my suit, I was going to yell for you but someone pushed me Mathew. Mathew was already wrapping a blanket from the small cabin around Alicia, we have to get you out of these wet clothes. He took her down stairs into the small room below he sat her on the small bed he used when he was guiding an expedition. He took the blanket and undressed her, she was shivering and was blue from the water. He took his wetsuit off down to the waist and wrapped his body around hers. She immediately felt the warmth and her shaking eased some. Once she had stopped shaking, he found her some of his clothes to wear and made her some coffee. It was a small boat but it did have basic amenities, a bathroom for one. She was happy about that and wanted to know why he hadn't told her before. Once she was good and warm he sat down next to her and asked if she could remember anything else about the guy on the tape and if she saw the person that pushed her in the water. Start from the beginning and tell me everything.

 I was in the tent going through the footage from my cameras and I was actually getting disappointed because all I had seemed to capture was small fish. Then I noticed a shadow on the lens and thought it was just a plant or scum that had drifted in front of the camera, I started to turn it off not thinking I was going to see anything else, and that is when I saw him. At least I think it was him. I looked more closely and saw what looked like the imprint of a gun beneath his suit under his arm, which is when I heard the noise from outside the tent. It took me off guard because of what I was watching and I ran outside without my shoes and saw the person running around the back of the tent into the trees.
 Did he have a wetsuit on?

No, he was wearing all dark green canvas like clothes and big boots.
Did you see a gun?
No all I saw was the back of him and he had some type of belt on with stuff stuck in it like a utility belt or something. It had some kind of gold rings on it too.
That sounds like he was prepared to walk down a cliff on a rope if needed, he must be trained in this type of terrain. We need to go back to camp we will be safer there where we can use your cameras to see around us. Do you think he knew your camera was there or did it look like he just bumped it by accident?
I don't think he saw it because when he looked at it was as if he was looking right through it.
Here get into this wetsuit while I pack a few things, we need to take as much as we can with us, it may not be safe to come back to the boat for a while. I know it's gonna hurt your scrapes but we don't have time you treat you here. We will take care of your scrapes and cuts when we get to the shelter. Mathew wouldn't it be safer to go back to the main island?
No being in the water alone with no where to go is not safe in case the people that are trying to hurt you comes back, its too long a trip back to the main island. We would be like sitting ducks, did anyone

know you were coming here besides the people you work for?

Well I don't think so, I didn't tell anyone. I really don't have anyone to tell I pretty much stick to myself and to work. I did have to go through a travel agent, our lady that usually handles all of the arrangements was out on medical leave.

Who did you use, a big firm?

No it was a small office on the north side of town, one of the guys in our department recommended him, why?

That could be your leak, who is this guy does he know you very well?

Actually, I use to date him, but very briefly, he could not accept the fact that I made more money than he did. We stopped seeing each other but he seemed ok with it, I mean we don't talk much but he is in a different department, actually, I hadn't talked to him for several months when he came to me to offer the information about this agent. I assumed he was only up in my department because he wanted the assignment himself, and then when he heard I got it he wanted to come along. He even came to me and suggested that we try again, for me to go to the boss and tell them I was taking him along with me. I told him no and he said he would persuade them to allow him to go on his own and we would work this out. That is one of the reasons I made it very clear to my boss that I would only go if I went alone. I am his best researcher and so he agreed. I heard that Nick was very upset when he found out what I had done, but I don't think he would want to hurt me. He doesn't seam like that type of person. He was never violent and I just don't see him as the type to know how to get around virtually undetected.

How long were you together and how long ago? What is his last name? What is his birthday? When did he start with the institute, and where is he from?

Why is all that important? And can you write that down, I mean that is a lot of questions. Why do you want to know Mathew, because of everything that is happening or because of you and me?

Look I don't like to think about the fact that someone else has been with you but that is not my reason for asking. We need all the information we can get to find out who is after you and why, if I'm going to keep you safe I have to know all the facts so don't leave anything out. If you don't believe me we can leave our

" thing" in the past!

I just want you safe.

Fine!! Because a " thing" is all it was to me too! Alicia turned away from him and started packing whatever she could put her hands on. She was so humiliated and so … sad. She had been a fool to think that what she had shared with Mathew had been anything more than sex for him. Why did she feel so terrible, she didn't want anything more than that, did she? They packed all the supplies they could fit into the four floating chests in silence. Alicia packed two of the chests with food and Mathew packed the other two with supplies. He packed ropes harnesses, a knife set he had forgot he had on the boat, it wasn't his favorite but it would get the job done if it came to that, he was not going to let anyone hurt Alicia. It made him cringe to let her believe that he didn't have feelings for her, but he wasn't going to tell her he was in love with her. That would have been a disaster, she didn't love him, or did she? It really didn't matter at this point he didn't need the distraction anyway, he needed to concentrate on keeping her safe . She was upset about what he had said, I guess Ill find out eventually what feeling she has for me, if any? He finished packing putting the knives in a place she couldn't see, he still had the 9mm gun but his skills with knives would keep them safe on the journey to camp. The Knives were quiet in case of more than one assailant, he didn't want her any more afraid than she was and he wasn't sure how she would react if she saw that he thought he needed a gun. Especially since, she had been so afraid of the gun that the assailant was carrying. He packed a sleeping bag designed to withstand the cold and an instant heat pad just in case. He liked the fact that they might actually have to sleep in that bag together. It was only made for one person but it would be big enough for the two of them but they would have to snuggle close, it would be good for the body heat. That's what he would tell her, it was the truth but she was so mad at him she more than likely wouldn't care. She would want her own. He had another one but he was not taking it with them, it would take up too much room. They finished sealing the chests so that the items inside didn't get wet. Matthew made his way over to Alicia while she was finishing up, he noticed the way she was struggling to move with the wetsuit because of her cuts so he told her to sit down and take down the wet suit so that he could clean and dress the cuts on her feet and legs now. Mathew really would have liked to wait but he could see it was causing her a lot of pain so he decided to do what he could on the boat. She just looked at him with those beautiful eyes full of hurt and anger, she didn't say anything she just sat down. She would have protested to him touching her at all but the cuts were really starting to bother her. She didnt think that they were too bad but they were stinging pretty bad and she knew that she needed to get them cleaned, she didn't need to get an infection out here.

Mathew opened the first aide kit that was always on his boat and started to look at the cuts, he rinsed them with saline first and then applied an antibacterial ointment to the cuts on her feet. They were not so bad, but she did have one good gash on her leg. He cleaned the cut, applied the cream, then wrapped it in gauze, and then waterproofs bandages. He didn't want it to get wet or let any bacteria form. He might have to give her stitches when they got back to the camp where the big kit was. Alicia had put back on the extra wet suit when he had finished and was ready to go. She had put on some of Mathews shoes that he had on the boat, they were too big but at least her feet would be protected as they made their way back to the camp.

 He pulled his wetsuit back up over his shoulders and tied the rope on to the four chests. He tied on one of the ropes around Alicia's waist and two around his own. Mathew put the chests over the edge of the boat and jumped in he then helped Alicia over the edge. They made their way back to the island slowly, Mathew didn't want to hurt Alicia's scrape and cuts from the rocks. When they got to the island, he untied Alicia from the ropes and retied all of the chests to himself and they walked back to the camp pulling the chests. Once they were at camp, he walked around the camp and looked inside before he allowed Alicia to go inside. He found nothing but was un-easy for her safety. Once inside he put the chests in the big room and told Alicia to take off the suit. She glared at him and went into the other room,

I be damn if he's gonna see me again! I don't know what the hell I was thinking feeling anything about this man that just wanted a good time. I can just have a good time too. Who am I kidding I like this man way too much to just have fun, I don't know what to do now except to just ignore him. If I talk to him, I'm just going to let him see my emotions and that it not something I'm prepared to do right now and maybe not ever.

He followed her in the bedroom and she just stared at him, he could not handle this he would have to tell her something. Look Alicia, I don't know what you are thinking but I do like you, It wasn't just sex for me, but my main concern is your safety and if we have to stay clear of each other for me to keep you safe than that's how it will be.

Now how am I going to make her believe that I really do care about her? I cannot just come out and tell her, she would not believe me now even if I did because she thinks I used her. This would be so much easier to protect her if I had not fallen in love with her.

What about my feelings Mathew? Does it even matter to you what I want?

"What do you want Alicia, because the entire time we have been here I haven't heard you voice your

opinion on us or what you want, so are you finally going to tell me because I would love to hear it!"
 She looked at him and just turned around so that she didn't have to face him, she didn't know what she wanted but she did know she didn't want to lose the closeness they had shared while on this island. What was she suppose to say, she couldn't tell him how she felt he didn't feel the same way. She didn't know if she could handle the rejection, with Nick it was different. She didn't love him, they had an understanding. They were not in it for the future, she knew exactly where they both stood, but with Mathew, she trusted him.
 "Alicia… look at me, what do you want from me?" "Look, I will take this in whatever direction you want, I don't want to push you but I like having you close to me."
 He reached for the back of her neck and she flinched.
 "You can trust me Alicia, I would never hurt you."
Inside Alicia felt the power of his words and she believed him but how could she trust her heart? How did she really even know if she loved him, she didn't exactly have experience in that department.
I'm going to help you out of your wetsuit now, ok. She just nodded, she didn't want to face him so she leaned back towards him. He pulled it off slowly trying not to hurt her. She winced as the suit peeled

away from her cuts. It seemed as though the cuts were hurting more now than before.

"They didn't hurt much before but now they are very sore. I don't know why they are hurting so much more now?"

"I have seen this before, you must be allergic to the spores that collect on the volcanic rock under the water at the edge of the island. Come on we need to get you in the shower."

He peeled off the bandages and then he gently wrapped a towel around her and easily lifted her into is capable arms. She wrapped her arms around his neck and leaned into his chest not protesting at all, she really could have walked but she needed to feel him close to her.

He carried her outside to the shower and deposited her in the small tent. He turned on the water and checked the temperature. He took her towel and put her under the lukewarm water. "We need to wash your cuts and scrapes and then put an antibacterial cream on them that has an allergy medicine in it. I didn't have it back at the boat but it should help with the allergic reaction and make you feel better. We also might have to stitch up that one cut on your leg, it is going to sting I'm sorry. Are you afraid of needles?"

"No not really, I can handle it."

It did sting but she could handle it if he was the one with her. He rubbed her scrapes and cuts gently with his hands under the cool water. She tried not to cry but it was more painful now then when the rocks had cut her. She looked down and saw red stained water at her feet. They must have been worse than she thought them to be. He spent a long time on her back, when she had been pushed, it was as if she slipped down a hill so her back was the worst, he hadn't noticed the scrapes there earlier. He was concentrating on getting her warm and then tending to the scrapes on her feet and legs. "Why didn't you tell me you were hurting on your back?" She had a long gash on her back that reached from the top of her thigh to about midways up her spine. He was picking out tiny pieces of rock that had been left behind and at the same time had one hand on her other hip caressing it.

"I didn't feel it earlier I guess I was so shaken from everything going on I didn't even notice." If he was trying to take her mind off her back, it was working. She had to close her eyes because the blood stained water made her a little dizzy. She wasn't afraid of needles but the sight or smell of blood done things to her. He felt her waiver and so he turned her around and made her look at him, her eyes were a little glossy. He turned the water off wrapped her in the towel and picked her up and carried her back to the tent. He dried her off the best he could and laid her down on the bed on her side careful not to touch her back. The scrapes and cuts everywhere else were small with the exception of the one on her leg. He unwrapped her and looked at her back, he went into the other room and grabbed the big first aid kit that had been in the airlift package sent by Alicia's company. He had noticed it earlier when they had un-packed. He was glad that they were responsible enough to think ahead and prepare for almost anything. He took out this purple looking cream and rubbed it generously on the cut on her back. She flinched at the pain and he sucked in a big breath, it hated to hurt her but had to make sure she didn't get an infection. He covered it in gauze and taped it in place. He laid her back so that he could take a better look at the gash on her leg and decided that it did need a few stitches.

"Alicia, this will hurt but only for a second. I have some numbing cream that works really fast, it only needs just a few stitches so it won't take long."

Alicia tried to not think about the blood it just made her woozy and sick to her stomach.

'Are you sure you know what you are doing, I mean your not a doctor or anything."

"I have done this many times before when I was in the military, which is where I went to school to be an investigator. We all had to take basic life saving skills classes before we went into the field."
Mathew started rubbing the cream on the back of Alicia's leg and had her laying on her stomach so

that she didn't have to watch and to give him easier access to the cut. He talked to her the whole time trying to keep her mind off of what he was doing .When he was done he sat her up and gave her a purple pill to take.

"What is this?"

It's a very strong allergy pill, you're allergic to the spores and that could make you very sick.

"Are you having trouble breathing?"

' No but I am so tired.'

Ok, I will leave you to get some rest.

"Mathew?"

Yeah… will you stay with me? Please? She didn't want to be alone, she was feeling no pain but she still felt dizzy from the smell of blood and very tired from the allergy pill. At this point, she didn't really care about the animosity between them, she needed him.

Ok but only, for a few minutes, I have some things I need to do. He laid down beside her and she nuzzled into his chest and was out in minutes. He laid there for a while just thinking about her, and then eased himself out of the bed. He needed to make this place as safe as possible, he didn't know what or whom he was protecting her from but he was determined to find out.

He went into the other room and opened the chests. He pulled out his perimeter ropes that he usually used on expeditions to detect large game that might be a threat, he always keep it with him. He would set a perimeter around camp and use Alicia's underwater cameras to see around in the water. They had only found one of the cameras that he knew of and they had installed eight, so he should be able to keep an eye on the perimeter of the island fairly well. That is unless the man in the water did notice the camera and deliberately took it out of commission. If that was the case then he could have looked around and found the others. Once he set the lines around camp, he would check her footage to the rest of the cameras and see if he could find anything else that might help him decide who was trying to hurt Alicia, and make sure none of the other cameras had been found. It took him a couple of hours to set up and when he came back, inside he checked on Alicia and she was still sleeping. He went to her laptop and sent his friend another email about what had happened, and to see if he had figured anything out on Alicia's friend Katie.

Alicia was attacked today, she was checking her camera footage and saw someone and she ran to find me and someone ran around the back of the tent. She ran to me, I was on the boat and someone pushed her in the water. She's ok but she didn't have a wetsuit on so she has a couple of bad cuts. Please get back with me as soon as you can, I think maybe this is all linked. I can't think of any other reason why someone would want to harm Alicia. Her job does not pose any threats to anyone or the animals and we didn't have any problems until we started looking for Katie. Let me know thanks man.

Oh yeah I need you to check out a possible person of interest that might be involved, she had an old boyfriend that had practically insisted on coming to the islands with her, he also set her up with the travel agent she used to get here. His name is Nick Rollins. See if you can find anything on him too. Again, thanks I owe you one.

Chapter 9

Alicia was sitting by the fire that Mathew had built
outside their camp, he thought that the light would
deter anyone from coming close to the fortress he
had made out of the supplies they had. She was
drinking her coffee and thinking about Katie.
Wishing she could remember more, something that
would help find her. She was trying to think back
to the day Katie came and then the weeks
following. She could remember Katie warming up
to her and talking to her. Katie was sitting on the
bed in the room they shared, it was about as big as
a washroom with the one small window. It was
always pretty dark in there and smelled a little like
old pine needles and dust. They did have their own
beds, only because that was one of the few
requirements the government had for foster parents,
but after a while, Katie started crawling into my
bed. All of a sudden, Alicia started thinking out
loud remembering some of the details of her
childhood with the foster home, Mathew was
careful to stay silent and just listen.

 "She was so little and scared….. she was always so
scared."

 She didn't talk about her life before the foster care
home with the Collins. Life seemed to pass by very

slowly without much change, I remember reading a lot she thought to herself. "Checking out books from the library at school was about the only thing that helped me get through the days, it helped to pass the time when I was at home. I remember reading to Katie about nice things, happy things and sometimes she would smile at me but not very often. Katie was a lonely sad little girl, she wasn't in school yet and I hated leaving her to go but at the same time I loved being out of that house away from those people. Sometimes when I came back from school Katie would be staring up at the walls and the pictures I had drawn and hung up. She would sit on the bed under the little window trying to feel the breeze from outside."

The foster parents were mean, they gave us very little to eat so I would sneak snacks to Katie, sometimes I would hide food from school in my backpack to give to Katie that night, crayons and paper too. I wanted her to have something to do when I was at school. So maybe she wouldn't have to leave our room during the day when I wasn't there. I remember this one morning Katie crying , begging me not to go to school that day. I wanted to go so badly but I couldn't leave her when she was so upset. She was my only family, I told Beta I was sick and she said to go to school anyway but jack came in and said to leave the girls alone, let them stay home. I wondered why he took up for me

when he never even spoke to us really, but I didn't say anything. Beta worked at the dinner down the street, and so she didn't argue she just left.
"What was it called" Mathew spoke up.
 I don't know at what point I stopped thinking my memories and started telling my memories out-loud, but I answered his question and went on. I wanted to the bottom of this. I think it was called the Roberts dinner, anyway beta left for work about an hour after I was to be at school and it was just me Katie and Jack in the house. I was nine and Katie was five, we were in our room where we stayed all the time because the Collins didn't want us with them, we rather be together and not with them anyway. We were both a little scared of them. Now that I think about it, the night before Katie had seemed different when I came back from school. She wasn't talkative to begin with but she did talk to me but not that night, she just sat there all evening and listened to me read without uttering a single word. I just thought it was her being her but now…I don't know it makes me think that something was bothering her. Later that morning Katie and I was hungry so I sneaked downstairs to get something for us. I thought I could make it to the kitchen and back without Jack noticing I was down there. He was downstairs watching the TV and it was somewhat loud. Katie was in our room waiting for me, she didn't want me to go but I

knew she needed to eat. I got to the kitchen and
started getting some cheese and crackers out, it was
the closest thing to me and I wanted to hurry. I was
almost to the stairs when I heard Jack call out my
name. He was sitting in the lime green chair that
was positioned in front of the small TV in the
living area, if that's what you wanted to call it. The
entire house was in need of repair maybe a
bulldozer would have been better. Anyway, I
stopped and put the food behind my back and
meekly called out yes sir. He told me to come to
him, I told him I just wanted a drink of water can I
please go back up to my room I'm still not feeling
very well. He said to come to him right now, I
think the whole block could have heard him if we
had been in a neighborhood where anyone would
have cared to listen what was going on. I was so
scared I think I may have wet my pants a little, I
carefully sat the food on the table in the hall so he
didn't see and I walked to where he was sitting and
stood a couple feet away from him. At first I didn't
really know what I was seeing but it didn't take me
long to figure it out. He was watching something
on TV, I couldn't see what it was but I could hear
it. I t wasn't something a young girl should see at
all, my eyes fell to the movements of his hands in
his lap. I was so young at first I didn't even know
what he was doing what was going on, but I did
know it didn't seem right. I had been very young

when my parents died and no one who cared to tell me things. He smiled at me and told me to come closer, I didn't move. I felt like I was frozen and I couldn't do anything, I didn't understand what was going on. He shifted in his chair where he could reach my arm and pulled me closer, he sat me on his lap and finished. I could here Mathew's breath catch in the background of my thoughts. He didn't touch me or make me do anything, he just made me sit there and watch. After he was done he pushed me off and said nothing, I ran to my room as fast as I could go picking up the crackers that I had dropped before. When I got back to mine and Katie's room she was waiting for me, I said nothing of what happened I just gave her the food I had in my hands. I didn't eat, I remember thinking to my self that this must be the reason for Katie insisting that I stay with her that day. I lay awake the whole night trying to figure out what to do, I could not leave Katie in that house another day without me to protect her. When I knew that they were sleeping, I packed a bag for Katie, and me and then we did it, we snuck out and never went back. I had met this lady at the public library, I had been there once or twice with the school and she was nice. We found an abandoned building, I don't remember what it was but we stayed there for the night and then in the morning we went to the library to find the nice lady. I can't remember her name, but when we got

there, I told her the whole story. I didn't know if I
trusted her not to send us back but we didn't have
any other choice. When I was done telling her the
story, she was crying and took us to some other
woman's house. We stayed there for a long time
maybe a week or so and then they put us on a bus
for a really long time and then on an airplane. I
don't know where we were but it was somewhere
nice, I remember thinking it smelled nice. That's
the last time I remember seeing Katie. It's like my
whole life between there and college was a blur I
was sent to another foster type home except this
one was nice, crowded but nice. I asked them about
Katie all the time but they acted as if they didn't
know who I was talking about like they never even
knew about her. I didn't understand it, they were
grownups they should have known what happened
to a 5-year-old girl. I do remember once when I
was a teenager that one of the other girls said that
she had had a sister once, and that she was told she
could never speak of her again. Like it was some
big secret, she said that they even changed her
name. That was the one big rule of the house never
talk about your past because it was behind you they
said, you have new lives now so speak only of your
future.

  " I'm sorry Mathew that is all I remember" I wish I
could remember more " how are we ever going to

find Katie when the last time I seen her she was
only five years old?
" We will find her Alicia"
You know, now that I think about it they never
changed my name but they always called me Lisa,
from the first day I got there. I had always thought
that I finally had a nickname, maybe they did
change my name and I just never really noticed. I
remember writing Lisa Valamos on all my school
papers, so maybe they did change my name and I
just don't remember my real name after all.
Mathew maybe the biggest problem is not that I
don't know where Katie is maybe I still don't
know who I really am.

Chapter 10

Beta and Jack Collins both grew up in the states and moved to England in the early seventies to become foster parents. They received a call from a friend who told them of a money-making opportunity. Beta and Jack Collins neither one came from good families, and lived in the seedy part of queens. Beta met Jack when she was 22 working in a strip club as a waitress, not that she was all that pretty. Beta was not ugly but had a homey type appearance she was a very self-conscience girl who had no confidence. Jack came in every night and spent all the he money had on booze and women, although that was never very much. He worked as a mechanic at a hole in the wall shop for a few hours a day. Beta was not a bad person but just seemed to have really bad luck in life and bad taste in men. Betas father was never in the picture apparently had disappeared the minute he had found out that her mom was pregnant with her and her mom well she tried but just was not a good parental figure. She did love Beta but she also loved drugs and they ended up getting the best of her so Beta was on her own most of her life. She didn't think much of herself so she usually ended up with losers that only wanted to use her for one thing or another. She hooked up with Jack one night and the two got married shortly after. He wasn't the best catch but he had asked her to marry him when none of the other men that she had ended up with had, she wasn't sure that would get the chance again so she married him for lack of a better offer. She should have known that once they were married he wouldn't change he still went to the club every night drinking and watching. Jack had an obsession for women, but he was also very controlling. Jack only let Beta work on the nights he was at the club, oh, he didn't care if other men talked to her or even messed with her. He let it happen right in front of him, he just wanted to be there to see it. He didn't take up for his wife at all, not even when some drunk was fondling her at the club, he got off on it. Beta was so spineless when it had come to Jack, she did what she was told and ignored the rest. It came from being told she was nothing as a child and growing up believing she was worthless. She had no self-confidence and no self-esteem. Jack pushed her around and took what he wanted when he wanted, and even brought home other women and took what he wanted from them with Beta in the house. Sometimes he made her watch, and she did because that's what he wanted. This was her life and she just accepted it, as if someone would accept a Pepsi instead of a Dr. Pepper. They had been together for about fifteen years when a friend of jack's called them up and told them about the things going on in London. He said that their was easy money to be made all you have to do is look after a couple kids that don't have parents. The state gives you money for letting these kids live with you. They don't check criminal records and all you need is to furnish them a room. Beta really had no say in where or what they did so when Jack said they were moving and why she didn't argue although she didn't really like the idea of having more mouths to feed. After her and Jack had been married a while he stopped working and it was up to her to bring home what little money she could and most all of it went to his drinking and partying anyway. They had nothing , and she never had anything for herself. Beta moved with Jack to London that same month, got in touch with the department of child services, and became foster parents that same year. Beta thought that things might change for them, she thought that having kids in the house might make Jack softer, but she didn't hold her breath waiting for the change. She never had really wanted kids but if taking care of these kids made jack different and would help her work less, she would do it. She went with jack to the meeting after his friend had set them up, she didn't say anything jack handled it all. They didn't have to do much just provide their address and names, and the lady told them that they would have a couple of kids ready for them in a few days, their were so many kids in need of homes back then. They had a couple of kids placed with them and started getting money, Jack found a club nearby witch is where he spent most his time, Beta noticed that nothing much changed and jack had her get a job to support his habits. Beta took a job at a dinner down the road and settled in, what else was there for her to do. They didn't really care about having to put up with the kids because they weren't allowed to come downstairs when they were home. Eventually the kids ran away and the money stopped. Beta didn't know why the kids ran away but didn't think too much about it. They ran away right after spring break, they were home all week with jack while she was at work. The checks stopped that first month after they fled and jack was mad at Beta for not having money for him to go to the clubs. Beta didn't make as much as she had made in the clubs in the past years. She was older and had gotten plump so the club scene had left her behind. Jack had Beta go down town and make a request for new foster kids and that is when they got Alicia. She was a quiet little thing that kept to herself. She was in school so they didn't see her too much. A year or two later they were stuck with another girl, and she had to be there all day. She wasn't old enough to go to school yet. One afternoon Beta had an idea that something was going on with the girls because the little one cried everyday when Alicia left for school, this morning Alicia said she was too sick to go to school and stayed home against Betas wishes, but Jack insisted to let the girl stay at home. Beta went to work but came home early only to see Jack through the window doing ugly things in front of the oldest girl. Beta realized that the little girls had been getting abused by Jack and although she was not what you call a standup citizen she could not stand by and watch these girls be abused like that, she couldn't. That night she left the windows and doors unlocked and hinted to the oldest girl of this fact, hoping she would take the little one and run. When they got up the next morning, the girls were gone and Jack was furious. He told Beta to go down and get more girls that they needed the money. Beta confronted Jack about what she had seen and he came after her throwing her up against the wall in the tiny kitchen. The handle on the cabinet door was broken and pierced Betas shoulder. She fell on the floor to her knees and heard him coming at her again, she reached up on to the sink and pulled herself up and grabbed a dirty kitchen knife from the sink. When he came at her this time he saw her with the knife, she held it tight and when he hit her this time the knife went through his left arm. She made it out of the house down to the dinner where one of the ladies there took her to a clinic on the other side of town. She was ok the cut on her shoulder was not too bad. She barrowed some money from her co-worker, Nancy and left. Beta moved back to the states after that, she never remarried and never took in any more children. She didn't keep up with Jack, and didn't know what happened to him. She didn't care!!

Beta received a call from some detective in New York City just yesterday, and she told him this story. He was asking allot of questions about the two girls that had run away and about Jack's whereabouts. She told them all she knew but that wasn't much. She didn't disclose the parts of abuse, she was afraid that she would get into trouble and she didn't want anything to do with it or Jack. She had since started to work at a small town grocery store and she kept to herself. She lived in a small apartment in a not so good neighborhood, but it suited her ok. She didn't have much but she didn't need much. She did go to a club down the street sometimes to have a drink and to watch the girls. She liked watching the girls get hit on by all the low lives it reminded her of her time spend with Jack before the kids had ruined everything. He had been a cheat and a drunk but she did love him and didn't care about his activities. She was lonely and the call started her thinking about Jack more and more. One night after work, she went down to the club and found a place in the back next to a crowded table, so that she could watch. The place was dark and full of smoke. After she had been there for a while, she noticed a familiar face and her heart almost stopped. It was Jack, after all this time he looked the same except he had some gray hair. She just stared at him and then he saw her as well. She sat very still and watched him push the young girl off his lap and get up and walk towards her. She couldn't move she just sat there like if she was tied to the booth and when he stood in front of her all she could do was look up at him. He sat down beside her, put his hand on her thigh, and slowly slid it up her leg under her skirt until he reached her panties and just smiled. She was frozen to the seat. She couldn't move, something about the way he looked at her made her so scared and excited she couldn't tell which emotion she felt more. He continued with his hands until he felt skin and rushed his hands in her and she jumped. He was not gentle, he was rough and mean. She didn't have to put up with this treatment anymore, she thought to herself. She didn't need him anymore and it was finally in this moment that she realized that. She scooted away from him pulling his hands away from her, he still had not said a word. She got up and started to walk away when he grabbed her arm and slammed her down on his lap he held her with one arm and shoved his other hand up her skirt again, getting the feel he wanted. She grabbed the glass of whiskey on the table and splashed it in his face and he released her. She got up quickly and ran out of the bar. She was so proud of herself, although she had not spoken a word to him, she had sent a message that she didn't want him. In the next couple of days, she was reading the newspaper and he had been arrested for rape of a young college girl. The next day they found him in the cell of the county jail dead.

Chapter 11

Mathew was looking through the tapes of video and stills repeatedly trying to see anything that he might have missed to give him a clue of who this was trying to hurt Alicia. He had to find out something new to go on, he was about to lose his mind. It had been three days since the attack on Alicia and still he had nothing. At least there had not been any sign of anyone on the island besides them in the last three days but that doesn't mean that they were not being watched. It was a big island and he was not going to leave Alicia alone long enough to search it. He needed to go out today and canvas the island at least the areas closest to camp and make sure there were no signs of activity.

He wanted to make sure it was safe enough for them to go out in her tree top stands for bird watching. She was getting restless sitting around inside the camp and was soon going to sneak out on her own if he didn't take her.

" Mathew it has been three days my cuts are better, and I need to get some work done. Maybe whoever it was , wasn't even after me. Maybe I was just in the wrong place at the wrong time. I really need to get some work done besides you can come along and "protect me" she said this with a little smirk on her face. He had grown to love her attitude.

Meanwhile she wanted to work and I had to make sure she was as safe as possible.

" Alicia at least wait until I hear something from my contact, I want to have a little more information on this whole situation before we make any decisions that could possibly put you or me in harms way."

"Promise me you will not go out on your own."

"Ok but I need to get some work done so can you call him or email him or something, maybe move things along a little bit?"

I will try to call him but no matter how long it takes no going out on your own, we don't know who that was and we still don't know if they were after you, me or what they want.

"Ok deal"

Alicia went into the bedroom part of the camp and decided to take a quick nap, it had been very hot the last couple of days and the stress of everything going on wasn't helping. She hadn't really been feeling very well but she wasn't going to tell Mathew that, he was already driving her crazy. He was just trying to protect her, but he had become so over-protective since the accident that he hadn't even kissed her since then. She missed his presence in their bed, he didn't sleep hardly at all and when he did, it was while she was working on the camera footage. He didn't want to be found vulnerable by both of them sleeping at the same time. He was so busy protecting her that he was kind of ignoring her too, at least the way she needed him most. She got into a thin t-shirt and boxers, which is what she basically lived in these days because of the heat and laid down. She was thinking about Mathew and the day they had together before the accident when she fell asleep.

Mathew was in the next room doing some research when he received an instant message from his contact in New York.

Hey man, I found out some pretty interesting info on your girl and her sister, I also dug a little on that old boyfriend and the foster parents. You are not going to believe this shit!

Ok well spill it I have been trying to keep Alicia calm and out of danger but it's getting harder. She feels safe so she wants to go back to work. What did you find out.

Well Alicia was right she and Katie were split up when they were little, it was like some kind of underground safe house placing agency for kids that were abused or neglected by their foster parents. The lady at the library that Alicia mentioned was one of the leaders, so when Alicia told her what was going on she automatically got in touch with the others in her group and got the two girls placed with new parents. They always split kids up thinking that it would be harder for the foster parents or the foster agencies to find them if they ever came looking. Most of the time they didn't, they were mostly all in it for the money and there always seemed to be more kids that needed placing.

So did you find out where Alicia and Katie were placed?

They were split up, Alicia going to a nice home in England but Katie, you will never believe this. She was placed in a home on the islands, there where you are. I did not find a name but I did find the address. I will send it to you in a minute; I do not think that it is very far from you. On the other side of the island from the docks where you work, but I'm not sure. The info on the foster parents and old boyfriend are the most disturbing. After Alicia and Katie, left Jake received a new child. The boy was a couple of years older than the girls had been but he was much older in his mind. He had been through a lot and the old man Jake must have liked him because the way my source talked they were close like this kid was his own son. Ok get this his name was Nick Rollins! How's that for creepy, anyway apparently after the girls left the wife Beta moved back to the states and Jack and this kid grew close like real family. Beta never realized that Jack had another kid stay with him. She moved and left when she realized that Jack had been abusing the girls. She's no peach I did get to talk to her, but she's not that crazy either. She said that she hadn't heard from Jack since she left and I think I believe her. She did seem to be a little paranoid about talking to me. She didn't mention knowing about the abuse but I could tell that's why she left from our brief conversation. Anyway three days after I talked to her I saw on the news where this guy Jack had been arrested for rape and was found dead the next day in the county jail.

This Nick Rollins that Alicia told you about, she dated this guy?

Yeah, and your telling me that he lived with Jack!

Yes, he apparently brought him in after Beta left to receive money and wasn't expecting a ten-year-old boy. Anyway, I guess this guy Jack liked the boy because he kinda took him under his wing if you will, he taught him to be a real character. However, this kid was smart, he went to school during the day and made good grades and went out with jack at night and was with all kinds of girls by the time he was fourteen. He watched jack for four years talk and be with women. Jack liked the boy to watch, he was sick like that. The boy came from a very disturbing background and was clinically psychotic. Him and Jack got along apparently very well and they would go to clubs together and pick up girls, if the girls was willing that was fine if not they raped them. They watched each other and everything, these guys were sick man. It's like if Jack was training him or something. You know like serial killers train a replacement for when they are caught!

This Nick guy went to college and got a degree in research just like your girl.

So what is this guys story, does he know who Alicia is, I mean does he know that she had lived in that same house?

I'm not sure I have to do some more research, but I think he does. I can't believe she dated this psycho.

Yeah, for a little while. It didn't sound like anything too serious but if this Nick knows who she is, and that she and Katie was foster kids of Jack's. I just wonder what his angle is, what is it that he wants from her? It makes me sick to know where he has been and to know he was with her too.

You didn't!! You didn't get involved with this girl did you Mathew?

She's not just any girl, she's the girl I plan to marry!

What, man are you crazy? Ok look... I will try to find out as much as I can on this Nick guy, in the mean time you need to be very careful. I also found some interesting info on this Katie.

Well she was placed on the island, I told you that. She was in an ok home but she had some problems. She didn't finish school she dropped out and she got into a bad crowd. She was hanging around with some bad seed named Juan that had been involved in some major drug cartel in Mexico near Guadalajara. His family still lives in Mexico and deals in large amounts of marijuana. He smuggles it into the islands some how, and then is able to get it to other parts of the country by transporting it out of the islands with some type of fruit. I honestly don't understand why he hasn't been caught yet except that he probley has some local cops in his deep pockets. Anyway, this Katie was hanging around with him, and hasn't been seen in a while. One of the guys that I have been talking to was a friend of mine out of police academy and was on this guy Juan's case. He says that they do have undercover cops in places but that they have been under a long time more than two years and that they haven't really heard anything substantial from them in a while. I'm thinking that they may have turned, but I don't know.

So this Juan, is he still on the islands? Do you think that he has any connection to Nick Rollins?

Well, I'm not sure to tell you the truth, I don't think so at least I have found no links of the two anyway. I think that Alicia is right about Katie being in some kind of trouble but I'm not sure that it has anything to do with the problems you're having. I will keep checking and send you any information that I find.

Ok, I will be waiting for an update, I am going to give you Alicia's phone number just in case we have to leave here in a hurry and can't take the connivance of a computer. Her phone is more high tech than mine is and can get internet signal out here.

Yeah man you really need to upgrade!!

Until now, I didn't have a need! All right man, well I appreciate everything, and let me know when you have anything else.

Ok, no problem and be careful, we don't really know who your dealing with out there.

Mathew closed the computer screen and just sat there. He had
 So many feelings rushing through his head he could barely see. He bent over the desk and put his head in his hands. He didn't even know where to start to try to sort all this out. Mathew sat there thinking about all the information he had just been given and wondered how he was going to tell Alicia. Not only was Katie in trouble but that she had been toyed with by her ex Nick and that he was linked with a part of her past that she had blocked for many years because it was to bad to face. How would she react when she found out that Nick was just as sick as Jack had been all those years ago. Mathew sat there for what seemed like hours trying to fit all the pieces together to make since of what was going on and figuring out the best way to tell Alicia. By the time Mathew looked up it was about two in the morning and he was exhausted. He took a look one more time at the cameras, they were all fine and he went outside and checked the perimeter to make sure there had been no sign of anyone. Everything looked fine and the lights and fire outside was still going strong. He went back inside setting the can full of pie pan pieces by the door so that if someone or something moved the canvas door he would hear it. He decided to go lay down with Alicia, something he had not done in a while.

He needed to be near her, to calm himself so that he could get some much-needed rest and think clearly. As soon as he got in the bed beside her, she snuggled into his chest. He had her close to him many times before but there was something different about this time. Maybe it was because he had finally made up his mind completely, it was when he was talking to his friend.

She's not just any girl, she the one I'm going to marry!

He brushed the hair from her face and whispered so lightly that it was barely a whisper at all, Alicia, I love you!

Mathew closed his eyes and went to sleep.

Chapter 12

The sound was like a barrel exploding right beside my head, it was so loud. The minute I heard the bang I felt Mathew jumping up and running outside with only his boxers on. I got out of bed slowly scared of what I was going to see but needing to make sure Mathew was ok. Nothing had happened since I saw the man in the water and I was pushed in, not even any disturbance around camp at all so what could this be? I stood in the door- way of the tent watching Mathew run to the perimeter and seeing a mushroom cloud of fire and smoke coming from the edge of the island. I called out to Mathew, " What is that, what's going on?

Go back inside and get dressed, I'm right behind you.
I was shaking, what could have made that cloud of smoke. There was nothing on this island that could have done that? I went in and started pulling on a pair of jeans and Mathew came in behind me.

Dress in layers, two pairs of jeans if you can three shirts and pack a bag, as he threw a backpack at me. I caught it at my head and he kept talking, he was talking so fast barking orders. Pack light something you won't have a problem carrying on your back.

What do I pack? I had a lot more questions but by Mathew's actions and strong facial expression, I didn't think that he would take to my questions so easily right now so I tried to ask as little as possible and do what he said.
Non-perishable food, extra clothes, first aid kit and extra socks for both of us. Here is my bag pack mine too!
 Alicia grabbed both bags and started stuffing things in them, she was so nervous she was just basically throwing things in. Make sure you pack comfortable but warm clothes that we can take on and off easily. It's hot during the day and cold at night.

Mathew threw a flashlight to her and it landed on the bed right beside her, she jumped like if someone had hit her.
I'm sorry I don't mean to scare you honey but we have to move!

What are we packing for? My voice cracked, We can't stay here anymore, someone torched my boat and I don't want to give them the chance to trap us here. We have to get going and find a way back to the main island. It's not safe to stay here anymore.

YOUR BOAT? How are we going to get back to the main island? What are we going to do? My voice seemed to be failing me now, in my mind, I was shouting but it came out little more than a whisper. Matthew took a quick glance at me and walked quickly to my side.

Alicia, I'm sorry if I'm scaring you but honey we have to move and do it quickly. I don't want to lose any daylight time, the terrain here can be hard to manage in the dark not to mention the animals that we have to protect our self from. Sorry, there I go scaring you again, look, I will not let anyone or anything get to you no matter what, do you believe me?

Yes, Alicia whispered.

Matthew held her for just a brief second and let her go. He wanted to grab her hold her, make love to her and let her know everything was going to be ok but he didn't have that luxury. He would not ever forgive himself if he let something happen to her so he had to put his feelings aside and put all his attention in one place and that was making sure she was safe at al cost. Even if that meant ignoring her, she distracted him, he couldn't afford to let himself be distracted, that's how mistakes were made, and people got hurt.

Finish packing and I will fill you in on the way, we need to get out of here and get as far as we can before dark.

Alicia finished packing their backpacks and Mathew went outside to gather a few things he needed, he put his head back into the enclosure,

Are you ready to go?

Yes, just let me get my boots on. I will meet you outside.

Ok

Alicia finished putting on her boots and went into the front room where her computer was, she wanted to see if her cameras had caught a glimpse of anything around the boat when a pop up email was waiting on the screen.

The messages that Mathew had sent back and forth between himself and his friend from New York was still on the screen. Alicia read them and when she came to the bottom, she saw it.

She's not just a girl, she's the one I'm going to marry!

Wow, what is he thinking? How can he be so arrogant and say that he is going to marry me when he doesn't even really know me or know what I want. What if I don't want to marry him? I don't want to marry him…..do I?   Well at least I know that he does like me, at least what we've shared here has not just been sex for him.

 DO I want him to really like me? It was so much easier for me not to admit I love him when I knew he didn't feel the same way. Now there's nothing stopping us and, oh, wow I can hardly breathe.

Alicia you ready we really have to go!

Oh, um yeah sorry I'm coming. Alicia was almost hyperventilating.

Alicia closed the computer like she had never seen the messages grabbed the backpack threw it on her back, and left the shelter.

As soon as she went outside Matthew noticed her breathing and ran over to her, are you ok what happened?

I'm …..ok….just …pan..ic ….attack.

All he could do was look at her, she was fine after a few minutes and all he could do was hold her. He blamed himself how could he be so insensitive and rush her the way he was without even really telling her anything? Damn he had to do a better job than this.

Are you ok?

 Yeah I'm fine now , wow, I haven't had a panic attack since I was a little kid. That was kind of crazy.

Well it's all over now and we have to get moving if you're sure you're ok?

Yes, I'm fine let's go.

Mathew steamed through the wooded island like a truck on a mission with precision and grace, Alicia followed behind not doing bad herself. At least she was used to remote places and could fair pretty well herself when it came to navigating. She was sure on her feet and was very balanced although the speed was starting to get to her. She never was in a rush when she was out on assignment, she took her time and studied her subjects. She was far from being lazy but she didn't know how long she could keep this pace. They stopped to eat and Alicia was glad for the rest. She unpacked a small bowl of chicken salad she had made the day before and handed him some with crackers. They might as well have a decent meal at least once, she didn't know how long they would be out here with no refrigeration. They would have to eat non-perishable items the rest of the trip. The cool chicken salad was such a blessing, it was super humid and she was wet with sweat. She had pulled off a couple layers during the journey, tied things around her waist, and stuffed as many items in her bag as she could. Luckily, she was down to a tank top and pair of thin pants that she had put on as her first layer. It was more of pajamas than anything else but it was the coolest thing she had time to throw on back at camp. When they finished their meal they had packed back up, hurried off back into the thickness, and went for what she could only tell as only a very long time, she had forgotten her watch at the camp she was in such a hurry to leave. She didn't want to ask Mathew, she didn't want him to think she was tired or weak. She didn't like the idea of Mathew thinking of her as inferior. Mathew slowed as they got deeper into the interior of the island, it was getting dark and harder to

move through the dense vegetation. Alicia was glad they stopped but only because she was tired and starting to get cold now. She wanted to put back on a couple of her layers. Mathew found a little clearing and put down his big pack.
Alicia.. Stay here I'm going to gather some wood for a fire, we will need one tonight, and then he disappeared into the vegetation.

Alicia sat her pack down and just looked around for a minute, just trying to get a grip of her surroundings. She noticed that the grass was not as tall here and that some of it was kinda smashed to the ground like something had been lying on it. She went over to investigate and found what she thought to be some type of animal bedding. Probley some type of flightless bird given the distance inland from the ocean and the sizes of the bedding. It could have even been turtles, they got big on the islands. This was a good thing.. Birds usually give off a strong sent so as long as the nesting area wasn't too old the sent would detour larger animals.
Alicia was still admiring the beds when Mathew came back into the clearing with an arm full of sticks and small brush. He put them down and left again. He came back this time with some type of big leaved looking branches, it almost looked like a big fan.

Mathew are those for the fire?

No, these are for our shelter, they can be very helpful against the cold, you don't want to sleep right on the ground because of the cool night and insects.

Oh, yeah.. No, I don't treasure the idea of sharing a bed with insects.

Alicia took a pair of pants out of her bag and slipped them on over her thin ones. She then put back on one of the extra layers of shirts to cover her exposed skin. It wasn't cold yet but it was getting cool and bugs were starting to bother her a little. Alicia pulled out a little bag and got out a can of off

Mathew grabbed it out of her hands

Hey, why did you do that?

You can't use that

Well why not?

Because it has a strong smell and whoever is looking for us might get a whiff and , besides animals can smell it too. Here use this it will keep the bugs off you. He handed Alicia a small bottle that looked like it was for spraying water or something.

What's this?

It is a mixture of soybean oil, basil, and lemongrass. Its all natural, doesn't stink and it will keep the bugs off, just use it. Trust me..

He said it like I was fixing to jump off a cliff or something, it seemed like every word from his mouth was very serious and that wasn't very many, not since we left the camp. He was so focused on something, it's as if he couldn't relax even a little. Not even enough to say a whole sentence to me without almost sounding annoyed. Now I'm kinda thinking maybe I did something wrong or said something to upset him. Thinking back over the past several hours I couldn't think of anything, we haven't really spoken enough to get into an argument or anything. Oh well, guess he will eventually tell me or get over it, either way this was going to be a long night.

Alicia found a big rock at the edge of the clearing and sat on it to apply the spray Mathew had given her to ward off bugs. She took the extra layers of clothing she had sheded earlier and put all of them back on. Mathew had been right it was starting to get pretty cold.

Mathew came into the clearing one more time and set down the contents of his find. He started immediately with the fire. He made one big fire to the side of the clearing and then he started several very small fires around the rest of the clearing. Mathew's mind was racing with all the information he had gotten earlier from his buddy.

How am I going to tell Alicia that her ex boy friend was raised by that ass? How is she going to react knowing that he acted the same way Jack did and that she let a man like him touch her. I don't want to hurt her but she has to know, I have to tell her the truth about all of this.

Alicia was up spreading out the big fan branches over a patch of the clearing between one of the small fires and the big one. She took the sleeping bag out of Mathews pack, laid it out over the branches, and crawled into the bed. She had had a very long day and was very tired. To her surprise the bed was actually comfortable, of course it would not have mattered much she was so tired she could have slept almost anywhere. She was getting a little worried about Mathew, he had been working so hard the last few days, and hadn't slept very much at all. He had laid down with her last night for a few hours, it was the first time he had laid down with her in a while. He felt so good next to her, she missed him.

"Mathew"
Yeah, what is it?
Come lay down with me you need some rest!
I'm fine, I'm going to stay up and make sure no one or nothing bothers our camp, Ill be fine go to sleep.
Mathew was now occupying Alicia's rock on the side of the camp from earlier.

As tired as Alicia was she dragged herself reluctantly out of the sleeping bag and went to stand in front of him. Mathew come with me, don't make me sleep here in the middle of nowhere all by myself.

Really, your pulling that card Alicia, you know just as well as I do that you are perfectly fine. Why do you want to make things difficult?

I'm not, you are! All I want is to go to sleep and you won't let me because I refuse to sleep by myself out here!!

I feel bad but I have to get him in the bed somehow. If he doesn't want to touch me, its ok I will be good and keep my hands to myself but he needs to rest and unless I do something, he will sit on that damn rock all night. There is no telling what kind of day we will have tomorrow. At this point, all is fair game as long as I get him in this bed with me!

Mathew shook his head like if he was so annoyed with me and I just grabbed his hand pulled him to the sleeping bag as if I handy noticed his blatant annoyance with me.

We were snug in the sleeping bag it was big enough but we were really close. Mathew finally put his arm around me and I snuggled my head onto his chest. I was just relaxing and enjoying the rise and fall of his chest under my cheek and had my hand wrapped up in the curls on the middle of his thick chest. I was almost out and he started to speak.

Alicia, I need to talk to you about something I found out today.

"ok"

This is not going to be easy for you to hear nor is it going to be easy for me to say but you have to listen to all of it before you say anything. The whole way out here today, I have been contemplating on how I was going to tell you this and I have decided that the best way is just to come out and tell you straight. I know you are a very strong woman and you can handle this if anyone could.

 Me , I'm struggling with it a little more than I should but I can't help but think of you as mine now and It kills me to think of how this is going to effect you.

"Ok, Mathew you're starting to scare me just tell me

The stars were high and bright in the sky and it was a beautiful night, the moon was bright casting a shimmer across Alicia's face and he didn't want to ruin it but she had to know the truth.

Do you remember me telling you I couldn't get a lot of information from the national databases; well my buddy could possibly get us some information on your foster parents and Katie?

"Yes"

Ok well after the attack on you I sent my friend some more information and told him to check out all possibilities that could have led to someone looking out to hurt you and that would know you were on the islands. He found out that you and Katie had been lucky enough that the lady from the library was actually involved in an underground group that took care of children that had been abused. When they split you two up Katie was actually placed with a good family. She was placed with a family here on the main island.

 It was very hard for Alicia not to ask questions but she knew Mathew wanted her to listen to everything first and he sounded like he was having a heard time getting the story out so she was quiet although it was very hard.

She apparently got into hanging out with a rough crowd and ended up dating a guy that has cartel drug connections. My buddy is looking for more information on where she is now but this guy she's with is really bad news. Now about the guy from the cameras. Mathew looked very strained and heartbroken as he started speaking again.

We checked out the agency that sent you here and the information hasn't come back yet but we did find out some bad news. Mathew told Alicia the whole story about Beta leaving and Jack getting a new foster child. He told her about the boy and how Jack raised him and how he was just as bad as Jack was.

Alicia, That little boy that Jack raised just happens to be one and the same Nick Collins.

Alicia just stared at Mathew, there had to be some mistake she would never had went out with a man like that, she would have been able to tell.

He has to be wrong, this cant be true. I can't have spent time with someone like him and not know, I would have known. Alicia stood there stunned and starring off into space and Mathews voice brought her back.

"Alicia, are you ok, talk to me baby"

Your friend had to get the wrong data that can't be true, I would have known, Nick was no prize but he was nothing like Jack.

We think that he only got that job because of you. He's smart Alicia and he knows who you are. We think that he might be trying to get back at you for Jack. He loved Jack and thought of him as a father and I'm afraid to say he has a reputation with women just like Jack. They even had women together, look, I don't want to get into specifics but you need to know what you're up against and trust me that I would have never said a thing to you about this if I didn't believe without a doubt that it was the truth.

Alicia just laid there trying to process all the horrible things she had just learned, her sister was in trouble for real and the man she had dated was a monster. Alicia thought she had escaped her past when in reality she had never gotten away from it. She carried it along with her through all her accomplishments and the problems of her past was just sitting back behind the scenes of her life waiting for the right moment to strike. She felt nauseated and stripped of her personal space. Some how knowing that no one knew how she had grown up and how she had been treated in the foster home had given her strength and confidence. Now to know that someone she had chosen to have a relationship with no matter the extent made her feel cheap, dirty, ugly, completely lost and Oh my God Sick. Literally sick Alicia scrambled out of the sleeping bag holding her hand across her mouth and ran to the edge of the clearing where the trees were thick barely making it and heaved until she had nothing left on her stomach and then heaved some more. Mathew was right there holding back her hair from her ashton face.

Mathew turned Alicia around to face him, her hair still in his hands. He didn't say anything just stared at her touching her face with his free hand. Pulling her close he held her in his embrace like never before. At that moment he knew, they both knew that they were in love and nothing would ever be the same.

Chapter 13

Rubbing her eyes, Alicia woke up to a cool morning and Mathew was nowhere to be seen. Sitting up Alicia wrapped the sleeping bag around herself and looked in the direction of the trees. All the small fires had gone out sometime during the night but the big one closest to their bed was still quietly crackling and the warmth felt good on her face. The sun was glorious and for a brief moment, she had forgotten the horrific story last night that now felt like a bad dream. If only she could stay here with Mathew forever and she would never have to face the reality about her past.

"Alicia"

Alicia jumped at the sound of her own name; Mathew's voice was loud and booming this morning. He was coming from the dense trees surrounding the clearing with the sun shining on his beautiful face.

"Where were you?"

I needed a personal minute, where I am sure you need one as well, would you like some help? He had such a big smirk on his face

"No thank you, I think I can handle it on my own"

"Are you sure? Really I don't mind at all"

"I'm perfectly capable of handling MY MOMENTS on my own," Alicia was now giggling like a little school girl

When she finally stopped laughing she remembered where she was. Then she was groaning, she hadn't thought about the whole bathroom in the woods thing "ugh" She reluctantly got up and faced her fear and disappeared into the trees.

So where are we headed, I mean how are we going to get back to the main Island without your boat? There are some anglers from the main Island that fish near the other side of this Island. If we make it in time, we might be able to signal them. They come every couple of days, hopefully they felt lucky today and they will be fishing.
"And if their not?"
Well our only option is to wait it out, but I think we have a good chance as long as we get there before sun set. I really do not want to stay another night on this Island unless we have to.
If you have finished your breakfast, we need to pack up and get going.

It was mid morning and Alicia had already shed out of most of her layers, it had turned out be a rather warm day. Alicia was lost in her thoughts as was

Mathew. They had barely spoken two words since they left the clearing early this morning. It was easy with Mathew, she could tell him almost anything. However, it was nice too, that they didn't always have to talk. She could get lost in her own mind and didn't bother Mathew. He was confident enough in himself that he didn't need constant stimulation from her to function. Any other man she had ever been with was so incredibly needy, that it always took so much from her she got tired of them quickly. Maybe that's why she never really had a very long relationship. Men were excessively needy, but not Mathew he was different. They had a way of communicating that she had never had with another human being not even with family. It was as if she had known him forever, he knew when to talk and when she just needed him to listen. When she just needed his hand on her face or to be left alone. He was perfect.

"Ouch"

"Alicia are you ok, Mathew ran back to her side"

"Yeah just in lala land and tripped over that down branch, I'm ok"

"You need to be careful; I don't want you getting hurt"

"I said I'm fine hey when are we going to get to the other side? How much longer do you think?"

Were Here

Alicia looked up and stepping out of the trees, she saw one of the most beautiful beaches she had ever seen.

It was amazing; it was so peaceful and tranquil.

All you could hear were birds singing and the slap of the gentle waves that were rolling up on the shoreline. It was a picture out of a magazine. As they walked out onto the sand covered beach, she drew closer to the bubbles forming in the sand from the waves. Alicia sat down and took off her shoes; the sun was so warm that she decided to dip her feet into the salty water for a minute. Looking back, she saw that Mathew was lugging some big branches from the tree line making a big pile on the sand.

"What are you doing? Why don't you join me the water is amazing.

Alicia had expected the water to be cold so she eased her right foot slowly into the water to be pleasantly surprised by the warm water.

"Maybe in a few minutes I need to get a big fire started so that if the fishing boats come near they can see us"

Alicia couldn't understand why this side of the Island was so beautiful where the other side had all the volcanic rock covering its edges.

"Mathew"

"Yeah"

Not that I'm not enjoying it but why is there such a nice beach here, It shouldn't exist?

Yelling from across the sand, "We have so many tourists that want to come out to this Island every year that a few years back the locals decided to come out and construct a beach on this side of the island for the tourist. Bring in a little extra money by offering an exclusive day trip tourist spot"

"What happened, you said no one hardly ever come out here?"

"Yeah, once they had most of the rocks smoothed down and the sand moved from the interior of the Island they realized that the weather out here is too volatile and changes too fast to safely have tourist out here. Therefore, it ended up being a wash out of a project.

"Well since were here Mathew we might as well enjoy it"

Mathew had the fire going, came, and sat down on the sand beside Alicia where she had her feet in the water that was creeping up the beach from the gentle waves that were consistently coming in.

"Would you like to swim a little, take a look at the fish?"

That would be amazing,

Mathew stood up shrugged out of his shorts and pulled his t-shirt up over his head, and held his hand out to Alicia who was still sitting on the sand just looking up at him. She put her hand in his and

he pulled her up to her feet. Smiling at her, he
pulled her shirt over her head and UN fastened her
bra.

"What if the boats come, they will see me"

"We have at least a couple hours before they wing
this way"

Mathew put her hands on his shoulders for support
and he slid her pajama bottom style pants off her
curvy hips and down her legs. "Step out of them, he
ordered"

She obeyed; he took her hand and led her into the
warm water. They waded out to about waist deep
and he stopped to face her.

"You are so beautiful"

The sun was high in the sky now behind Mathew
shining rays of light on Alicia's glistening wet full
round breasts. He cupped them with is hand, they
are so perfectly round. He leaned down to kiss
them and she jumped.

"Alicia are you ok, I am so sorry baby I should
have known that after last night you wouldn't want
to be touched"

"No" Alicia grabbed his hand and placed it on her
breast "I want you to touch me" I want you to
touch me everywhere and do everything to me so
that all the memories I have are the ones of you
touching me.

Mathew was still cautious of there being someone
else on the Island but was paying attention and

didn't see anything out of place, and he didn't want to worry Alicia any more than she already was. Mathew lifted his hand and brushed Alicia's hair away from her face; he trailed his fingers ever so lightly down her soft neck to the swell of her breasts and circled her nipples with his rough thumb. She was so turned on all she could do was groan, she lent her head back and closed her eyes and just let go. She wanted to feel loved and wanted by someone that deserved to touch her. Mathew drew her up out of the water where she was straddling him. He carried her to the shore while ever so lightly trailing kisses down her neck to the swell of her full round breasts. Once out of the water he laid her on the sand where the water was still barely hitting them. Lying beside her, he took one nipple in his mouth and traced it with his tongue before gently biting it and tugging on it. He then did the same with the other.

Alicia with her head drawn back on the sand and her body curved off the sand toward his was moaning loudly with the bright rays of the sun on her wet skin. Slowly Mathew drew Alicia's panties off and his boxers as well. Laying Alicia back on the sand she could feel the grittiness of the sand and the warmth of the water on her butt and thighs. Mathew settled himself between her legs still kissing her breasts. Reaching for her sex, he found it with his eager hand, and gently slipped his finger

inside the warmth of her body. Alicia groaned lifting her hips to his hand wanting more. Mathew trailing kisses down the length of her body found himself exactly where he wanted to be. First kissing the inside of Alicia's thigh with his hands wrapped around and underneath her legs for a strong hold. He didn't want her to move. Moving closer he slid his tongue over her causing her to pant, he then had her in his mouth. Alicia wanted more she wanted to feel him she tugged on his head that was still between her legs. He raised himself over her and sunk into her steamy wetness like never before. They were one, and neither of them would ever be the same. For the first time in her life, Alicia felt totally and completely safe, wanted, and most of all loved. They laid on the beach together for about an hour, and realized that they should get dressed before the boats came around. Alicia had gotten dressed and was unpacking their bag getting out the package of dried fruit when she saw something out of the corner of her eye.
When she looked up she realized it was a boat, there was a boat!!
"Mathew" Alicia ran across the sand to where Mathew had been adding wood to the fire he had lit earlier.
"Mathew there's a boat"

Chapter 14

Mathew was off and running at full speed towards
the fire he had built.
Alicia stood there looking at him as if he was a
crazy person. "Mathew what are you doing?"
Alicia hurry, help me put the fire out"
"But Mathew the boat, I thought"
Alicia, hurry and help me, Alicia runs over where
Mathew is kicking sand all over the fire putting it
out. Alicia starts throwing sand on the fire but can't
help but wonder why.
The fire is so big that they are not getting it out as
quickly as Mathew wants; he pulls her by the hand
and starts running towards the cover of the trees.
Once they are into the trees and can no longer be
seen, Mathew explains with heavy breath that the
boat she saw was not a fishing boat but one of the
drug cartels. Probably picking up a shipment or
delivering, either way they wanted no part of it.
We have to run as far away from the edge of the
Island as we can, maybe we can make it back to
base camp before they catch up to us. We might be
able to defend ourselves there; did you happen to
grab our bag?
"No Mathew you pulled me into the trees I don't
even know what's going on"

Alicia they will see the fire on the beach, they will come looking for us, and they won't stop until they find us.

"But you said our only way off the Island was the fishing boats what do we do now, we can't just let them find us"

We are out of options Alicia, where is your phone? Its in my pocket, I put it there after we got dressed. Alicia dug in her pocket and found it. Held out her hand to Mathew "here"

Mathew opened it and out of sheer luck, it had a signal, He opened it up and called his buddy.

"Its Mathew I need a big favor, were in trouble." Mathew told him the compact version of the story about his boat and the cartel boat and then hung up the phone, once again leaving Alicia in the dark with his non-descriptive one sided phone conversation.

"What's going to happen now?"

It depends, we need to get back to the base camp as quickly as possible and get some extra clothes in case we are stuck out here a few days. I also need to get your computer and burn the hard drive.

"Why would you want to destroy my computer?"

"I don't want them to find it and have your contact information and we can't carry it with us its too bulky, we are going to be moving fast. They ran through the deep vegetation and that is when Mathew heard it.

Alicia and Mathew both stopped
 "get down"
Alicia and Mathew both crouched down low to the
ground. Mathew motioned for Alicia to come to his
side,
 "stay here and don't move"
"But where are you going?"
I want to see if I can tell what direction the sound
came from, just stay here."
Mathew moved low and quietly towards the base
camp in the trees, until soon he was out of Alicia's
sight. A few minutes had passed and still no sign of
Mathew. Alicia was already scared, now she didn't
know what to do.
 "Mathew" she whispered "Mathew"
But she got no answer, then suddenly from behind
she heard footsteps and as soon as she turned
around there was a rough hand across her face
preventing her from making a sound. She tried to
kick and scream but it was no use. Alicia elbowed
the man holding her and she was able to get out a
single scream before another man came up from
behind and smacked her hard.
Mathew was looking in the direction of the base
camp they had built only a couple of days earlier
when he heard a horrible sound, he heard Alicia
scream.
 "OH SHIT"

Mathew ran back as fast as he could, he hadn't gone very far. What was he thinking leaving her by herself knowing these crazy people were out here somewhere? If anything happened to her, it was entirely his fault. He would never forgive himself. He searched in the place where he had left her and there were no signs except that her jacket that she had been wearing when they ran from the beach; it was lying on the ground next to the fallen tree branch she had been crouched beside.

Mathew picked up her jacket

"I will find you Alicia and I will kill whoever is responsible for taking you away from me"

Mathew searched the area and went towards the beach where they had first seen the boat. Once Mathew reached the beach, he saw the fire and their bags that they had left but the boat and Alicia was nowhere to be seen. She was gone and they had taken her.

Why had he only heard her scream once, what did they do to her? Think Mathew think, where would they have taken her. Alicia still had her phone in her pocket from earlier. She had to because it was not on the ground and it wasn't in her jacket. That's good, that's really good I can track her with the signal from her phone. I guess the technology is not such a bad thing after all. Now just to get off this Island so I can trace her.

"These son of a bitches will wish they never laid eyes on her after I'm done with them"

Mathew spent the next couple of hours going over everything they had been through together in his mind trying to find a clue or something he may have missed to help him find her. He built the fire even bigger and went through all the things they had left behind that she had packed from the camp. He was gathering up the extra clothes when he heard a sound like a horn and saw a fish boat, just a few yards out. Mathew put the backpack on his shoulders ran into the water and jumped in. It didn't take him long to reach the boat, he was used to the water and was a very strong swimmer. When he reached the boat, he realized it was Hank. He pulled him up and asked what he was doing out here.

"I have a favor to ask, I need to get back to the main Island as quickly as you can get me there. I came out here with a woman, "Alicia" She is a researcher and we had some trouble on the Island. Someone blew up my boat and then we came to this side of the island to catch a ride with you. Someone on a big speedboat took her, I think it was cartel but I didn't get a good look. Do you happen to know anything about the cartel or where they hang out?

"I don't but I think I know some one who might be able to help you, but you should just call the police

Mathew. These people are bad news and you do not want to go up against them by yourself, you will end up getting yourself killed. How did the two of you get mixed up with them anyway, you in some kind of trouble?

"No, she has a past and apparently she brought it with her without knowing. I appreciate your concern but I can't go to the police with this, she is with them because of me, because of my mistake and I have to make it right. I have to find her before they do something to her I will regret.

"Well you know I don't know much I'm just an old fisherman but I will tell you this much, If you go in there with your head full of romantic notions for this girl. Neither one of ya is going to come out alive, you have to clear your head and think. I have a brother you know Gerald don't ya?

"Yeah I have seen him around"

"Well he pretty much sticks to himself these days cause of his rocky past, but right about now his past might help you out. Now he ain't real keen on talking about it too much but I think if we explain the situation, he will help you as much as he can.

"How is his past going to help me, I thought he was just a retired airplane mechanic?

He is but before that, he was a pilot for them airplanes he works on. He had one of those big fancy jobs of a private pilot for some big money fellow from the states. He had a nice setup too, good paying job, nice benefits. The man he worked for was always giving him bonuses for making deliveries for him. Boss didn't tell him what he was delivering, and he didn't bother to ask. I think that's why he always took such good care of him, giving him those big bonuses and passes to get into all these fancy places and always paying the tab. Well about ten years in, Gerald started noticing that his boss was adding security and never traveled alone and acting paranoid all the time. On one of his routine flights, Gerald was on the runway getting the plane ready for takeoff when he saw his boss drive up and as soon as he stepped out of the car, feds came out of the wood works and surrounded him. To tell you the truth I have no idea where they came from, didn't see or hear em until they had him. They took him and Gerald into custody for questioning. Ended up that Gerald had been smuggling drugs into the country and his boss was being blackmailed to do it. He was some hot-shot politician or something. Anyway, Gerald went to prison for accessory to drug trafficking. He got in good with a few cartel members in the pen. It wasn't what he wanted but it kept him breathing. Since he got out, he has kept his head low as not to piss them off and not to get into any trouble. He might have a couple cards still up his sleeve that he can pull to help you.

Gerald was a loner and was set in his ways but was a nice guy; he was just a little rough around the edges.

As soon as they had hit the dock, Mathew went to Gerald, and explained the situation and asked if he had any information that would help him find Alicia.

"I wish I could help you but I don't know what you want me to do?

"If you could just maybe point me in the right direction where I might find her or even just get a clue where to start looking I would owe you. Maybe they have a home base that they work out of, or a front that they use to work from that they may have taken her to.

"Well there is one place they could have taken her, there is a small Island only about twenty minutes boat ride from here, and they have a house on the interior of the island. I delivered there by boat once, it was normally not my place but something came up and they said jump so I said how high. Anyway, it's a big place but pretty well hidden from the passer by, belongs too the big guy. The one my boss works for, his name is Juan. I never met him but seemed like he was untouchable. I think I can still remember how to get there. If you want, I will draw you a map.

"That would be great"

Ill get that for you and Ill throw in a couple rounds
of ammo if you need it, my brother here says your
good people and they have your girl. This wont
make up for all the mistakes I've made but maybe
it will put a little dent in it anyway. Fallow me
down to the boathouse and we will see what we can
dig up for ya. I didn't do all those things for the
cartel and come back empty handed, maybe you
can use my "bonuses" and get a little pay back for
me too. Just be careful these people are dangerous
and they are mean. They don't give chances and
they are not afraid of the police, they own them so
you are on your own, I hope you can handle it.
"Thanks I appreciate anything you can give me; I
will get her back no matter what. I just hope I'm
not too late. I have a few things I need to take care
of; do you happen to have a computer and internet?
"No, I don't but Hank has one of those fancy
computers at his office. Don't ya hank? He says it's
to keep him organized on his fishing business but I
think he just likes to watch those dirty movies
(chuckles).
"Oh shut up Gerald" "yea Mathew I have one, we
will go down there as soon as yall finish up at the
boat house, I'm gonna go into the house and get a
beer yall want one?
"Count me in hollered Gerald, Mathew?
"No thanks I need my head straight"

Chapter 15

Mathew looked at his hand drawn map that Gerald had given him before he left. He studied it as his life depended on it. Gerald was very precise; he had made it to the outskirts of the island very easily and now was studying the part Gerald had done about the island itself and the house where he hoped to find Alicia. Mathew jumped into the water slowly as to not make any noise, of course he was far enough out no one should hear him anyway. He had found a rocky and heavily foliaged area that didn't have any clear beach to approach the island. This would allow him to hide his boat and make it to the interior of the island without being spotted. He wanted to have as little contact with anyone on the island as possible, once he was sure that Alicia was safe on the main island, then he would deal with the bastards that took her, or at least that was the plan. He didn't want any chances of getting Alicia hurt. As soon as Mathew was on the island, he was out of his wet suit and into all black and dark green military gear. He had folded the map he was given by Gerald and was on his way.

Alicia woke up to find that she was in what seemed to be a house out of the fortune 500 magazines she use to sometimes read. She was still groggy from whatever they dosed her with, whatever it was it had to have been strong. She had a pounding headache too and the right side of her face felt swollen, hot and pounding. They must have hit her to knock her out before they drugged her. She was in a large open style room with huge windows, but there was no light shining through. She hadn't been tied up, although she absent mindedly rubbed her wrist where it seemed as though she had been at some point. Alicia was trying to get her thoughts together, trying to remember what happened. She rubbed her hands down her legs and remembered her phone, where was it. She had put it in her shirt because she was planning to take some of the layers of clothing off. Alicia scrambled up and patted her chest until she felt it. She pulled out her phone.

"Yes"

she dialed the hotel she had been staying at and the front desk picked up. She didn't have a way to contact Mathew so she left a message for him at the hotel hoping he would think to check there knowing it was the only place she had been on the island. She couldn't call anyone from back home because in light of all the things she had found out in the last couple of days she didn't know if she should trust anyone, including her own judgment. Mathew, yes Mathew she could trust. He would find her, she gave the hotel a strange message but she knew Mathew would understand it, which is if he ever received it.

She was going to try to send an email to Mathew but her phone went dead. "Shit, are you kidding me?"

Alicia got up from the bed she was on; it was a huge four-poster bed with black and gold satin coverings. It was very soft and had netting on the top. She walked over to the windows and tried looking outside but the windows were covered with some type of dark tint, so dark you couldn't see out of them.

"Explains why there is no light in here, I wonder what time it is and how long I've been in here?" Alicia looks around the room trying to find a clock TV, anything that will help her figure out where she is but there is nothing. The room is very modern but no electronics of any kind. She makes it to the other side of the room, still clumsy and a little woozy from whatever they had given her. She pulls on one door and it must be locked from the outside because it doesn't budge, she walks across from the bed and pulls on the only other door and it opens to a very large and beautiful bathroom. Alicia enters and turns on the faucet, cool water runs into a black marble sink; Alicia splashes her

face with the water and tries to recover. The water
feels good and makes her see a little more clearly.
As Alicia looks at herself in the mirror, she hears a
sound in the bedroom. She turns around half hiding
behind the door not knowing what to expect. As
she rounds the wall and looks into the room, it is
not what she expected to see. There was a young
woman dressed in a very expensive, very showy
dress. It was black with a red satin tie right under
the bust line accentuating her breast. It was short
with the same red satin lace at the hem. The woman
was rather tall, long legs light complected and
blonde hair, which had clearly been colored at
some point because you could see some red in it.
She was beautiful and almost childlike in her face,
she seemed sad and disoriented. I took a step closer
and she backed away as if I was the one that had
her locked up and thrown away. She seemed so
much like a child and so familiar like I was having
dejivu. I could not quite put my finger on it and
then she spoke and I almost fainted. I recognized
her voice, how could I ever forget that voice. Yea it
was more grown up but in a way it sounded the
same, it was Katie. I was standing in the same room
as Katie, and for a minute, I forgot all about the
fact that I was being held captive in a strange place
against my will, about the bad men with guns and
about Mathew. All I could see was Katie as a little
girl and I practically ran to her side and grabbed her

in the biggest embrace I think I have ever given anyone in my lifetime.

Chapter 16

I felt her tense as soon as I touched her but I didn't care I held for anyway for what seemed like a long time. I stood back and held her by the arms just looking at her taking it all in. I had so many questions to ask her and then it all came rushing back, I staggered backwards almost landing on the floor catching myself by the facing of the bathroom door. I opened my mouth but it was so dry I shut it and swallowed.

"Katie, is it really you"

She was just looking at me as if she had seen a ghost; her voice was very meek and shallow and answered with only one word.

"Yes"

"What are you doing here and how are you involved with the men that locked me up in here. Have they locked you up too? But as soon as I asked the question I knew the answer, she was here on her own free will, why else would she be wearing the expensive clothes and have a key to the door that has me locked up?

"What is going on? Why am I here?"

Katie just looked at me

"How do I know I can trust you?"

"Because I am your sister, or at least we were for a while. Don't you remember me; I am Alicia we were in the same foster house when we were little."

"I remember, but you left me, how could you leave me?"

Katie may have grown up but her eyes were still a little girls eyes, she seemed so fragile.

"I didn't leave you, I took you to those people for help, I didn't know that they were going to split us up, they said you were safe and with a good family? What are you doing here and where exactly is here? What am I doing here?"

"The only reason you are still alive is because of me. I asked Juan to not harm you, at least until I got to talk to you and answer some of my questions."

"Katie, who is Juan and what do you mean only until you could ask questions, what is going on?"

"I have to go, I will have someone bring you dinner in a little while." And Katie left the room. I heard the door lock seconds after it shut behind her. I could have sworn I saw a big guy wearing black pants and shirt when she left, does she have bodyguards? Alicia was so confused with everything going on, she had such a big headache all she wanted to do was sleep, and since there was clearly nothing else to do she went and laid down in the big four-poster bed, and immediately sleep took her.

Mathew saw the house in the distance and he made his way silently through the underbrush and vegetation of the small island. As he got closer to the dim lights of the house he noticed there was a wire fence that blended in with the surroundings, it looked as thought it went around the entire place. Mathew thought that it was a hot fence so he was very careful to find a spot in the fence where he could get over it. It looked like it was more for the animals of the island than for intruders. It wasn't a problem to get around, just a little annoying. Once he was over the fence, he was careful to move slowly and quietly not to disturb anything. The closer he got to the big house the more he began to notice how the vegetation was out of control. There was moss or vines growing up all sides of the house and there was not a congenital yard. It was as if the island was trying to take back that piece of land house and all. Maybe they kept it that way to hide it, It was the perfect place to keep someone hostage without anyone from the outside world knowing about it. Alicia has to be in there, and I will find her.

He came up close and tried looking into a window but they were covered with some kind of dark tint that you could not see past. This would prove to make things a little more difficult, not being able to see what is there before going in. Mathew worked his way around to what should be the back of the house and found a dark wooden door; he listened at the door for what seemed like forever. Then finally heard voices, he couldn't quite make out what they were saying only that it was three different voices and it was two males and one female voice. Mathew slunk back into the vegetation as the voices got louder and then the door opened. The two males came out walked right beside him without noticing him. It was dusk so he was able to stay out of sight hiding in the dense vegetation that surrounded the property. He slipped a small piece of bush from the ground inside the edge of the door to keep it from locking. Once the two men left and was out of Matthews's field of vision he waited a few more minutes then slowly opened the door into the house. The inside was much different from the outside; it was very modern and very squeaky clean. He made his way through a spacious kitchen that seemed to be in constant use by the looks of it. He made his way out into the interior of the house and to the front of the home. To the right was a very big open space that looked to be some type of living area, but it was too clean, too…hard. It was as if it was made to look like a home but in reality, it was just a meeting place for something or a model. Not somewhere someone would actually live or spend any time. To the left was a dark hallway and to the front was a big straight staircase that t'd at the top going to the right and left.

Mathew crept slowly up the stairs, made a heat decision, and went to the right. Matthew passed multiple closed doors as he crept down the hall. When he reached the last door, he heard a slight groaning sound. As he continued to listen, it grew louder and he recognized it. That is Alicia; he knew she was having a nightmare. Mathew reached for the door but it was locked, he pulled a little pouch from his belt loop. One of the toys that Gerald had equipped him with, and soon he had the lock popped. He closed it gently behind him and that is when he saw her, Alicia was laying on top of a black and gold comforter in a bed moaning and groaning something about leaving.

"Alicia.....Alicia"

Mathew gently shook Alicia until she was looking at him, she didn't say anything just lunged at him and they both landed on the floor making a loud noise. Mathew put his hand over Alicia's mouth to quiet her, he pulled her to the door and tried to listen and find out if they had been noticed by anyone. Mathew drew in a silent breath as he listened and heard nothing. He bent down and looked at Alicia.

"Are you hurt, did they hurt you" Mathew searching her with his eyes and hands trying to find anything that might have bee physically done to Alicia. He found nothing and then finally looked up at her and she was crying.

"I knew you would find me"

"Come on, if your ok we have to get out of here"

"NO... Mathew I cannot leave, I have to stay…. Its Katie, she's here!"

"What, no Alicia we can't stay here, they people are very bad people they will kill us, we have to leave"

"We have to find Katie, we have to take her with us, and I can't leave her again."

Mathew quietly opened the door and looked down the hallway; he did not see anyone so he gently pulled Alicia behind him. As they went down the hall, they heard soft music coming from the other side of the hall.

"That has to be Katie, we have to go to her and take her with us. Please Mathew?"

As much as Mathew wanted to get Alicia to safety, he did not want to deny her a reunion with her long lost sister so they went towards the music. The closer they got the louder it became until they were finally right outside the door and it was not locked, it was ajar just enough to see Katie sitting on a small couch beside a big bed like the one in the room where Alicia was except everything was decorated in soft and inviting colors. There was a grand piano on one side of the room and Katie was there sitting looking at some kind of book. Before Mathew could stop her, Alicia had scooted around him and into the room. Mathew could do nothing but fallow as Katie or the girl in the room had already seen them, he still was not convinced that the girl in the room was Katie. How could it be, and if by some crazy chance it was, why was she involved with the leader of the cartel?

"Katie, please you have to come with us. This is Mathew and we are getting out of here."

"Even if I could leave with you, why do you think I would want to and how did you get out of your room?"

"Katie please, you said that I left you as a child I am not going to leave you a second time. You have to believe me that I never meant to hurt you; I didn't know they would slip us up when I got us out of that house."

"Look I don't know what you think you can do, Juan is very powerful. His reach is very far and even if I did leave with you, and we did manage to get off this island alive he would find us, he would hunt us down!"

Mathew steppe in "Katie right... Listen to Alicia, I know that this is crazy and that you are scared of Juan but let us try to help you. What do you have to lose, unless you want to stay?"

"Ok I will go with you, but we have to be quick Juan's men went to go and pick up Juan, they should be back any minute and there are still guards in the house. I can get us around them but getting off this island without them knowing it will be hard if not impossible."

Katie changed her clothes and gave Alicia some jeans as hers had been ripped when they had taken her.

The three of them made their way down the hall, down the stairs and in though the kitchen. The guards should be in the meeting room discussing the next night's plan, so they should have a few minutes to get out the back without being discovered.

As soon as they reached the kitchen door, a woman appeared from the other room. She just stood there and stared at them as if she did not know what to do; she was in shock and didn't know whom to trust. It felt like forever until anyone of us moved but it was only a few seconds. Katie turned toward her stood up straight and said, Maggie we are getting out of here. You can join us if you want, we will protect you. Maggie just stood there staring at Katie, at all of us like she was made of stone with her mouth dropped open, I guess trying to figure out if she should go or scream. Katie walked closer to her, "Maggie, please just come with us. I know you hate it here with all the guns and drugs. I know you want to go home to be with your family, think about it Maggie. Your daughter had her baby; you have a granddaughter and you could be spending time with her right now. Katie was trying very hard to convince the servant to come with us, she knew if she did not come with us she would have to tell everyone she had seen us and would ruin our chances of ever getting off this island alive.

"Katie, you know I can't leave and my family is why. Even if they didn't catch us, even if we were able to get off this island and go somewhere they could never find us. They would hunt down my family, they would kill my family! Katie I cant leave, and you know I have to tell them you did. I wish I had never walked in here and seen you. I will give you five minutes but then I have to tell them Katie, I am sorry honey. I really like you; you made this place bearable almost like a real home. I will miss you terribly."

Katie held the older woman tightly for just a second and then led the way out and we followed.

Chapter 17

Moving through the underbrush staying as low as possible to avoid being detected, Mathew made a motion and they all stopped. There were footsteps coming up fast behind them, it had to be at least three people or more. Mathew pushed the girls in front of him and they started running, Alicia fell down and Mathew turned back to help her up and a loud pop sounded right behind them. Alicia ducked and felt the air of the bullet pass right by her ear; she screamed and hit the ground. Mathew was already pulling her and running as she was screaming. Katie was right in front of them and did not seem as scared about the gunfire. Almost like she was use to the noise. It wasn't long until Mathew saw the place where he had hidden his boat earlier. It was dark so it would take a few extra minutes to get it out and ready to take off, minutes that they did not have. The cartel members that were after them would not give them the time they needed so Mathew rushed the girls towards the brush and told them what to do to get the boat ready. Mathew turned around and pulled the Mac-10 from under his jacket, took a few steeps back away from the girls and fired in the direction of the noise. It was just seconds and he saw the men carrying guns and firing in his direction. He ran away from the girls as to draw the fire away from them giving them time to get the boat and get in. Mathew hit one of them and then took a bullet in the thigh. The other two took cover to avoid Mathews mac-10, Mathew took the time to head toward the boat just a few steeps away. It was very difficult dragging his leg and then Katie was by his side helping him into the boat while the cartel was reloading. Mathew hit a button he had been holding on to since he first reached the outside of the house. When he first reached the property he had put a bomb on the underside of a vehicle outside the house, it would work as a good distraction to help them get out of there. About five seconds later, the four wheeled off road buggy blew and made a huge explosion. Gerald was right; this made a really big bang for such a little device. As soon as it went off the two cartel members that were still alive turned and saw the fireball, they fired a few more rounds in the boats direction and then headed back towards the house. The boat sprang to life under their feet while taking the last few rounds of fire from the other two guys. As soon as they were a little ways out Mathew slumped down into the boat only now did he start thinking about the bullet in his leg, Mathew knew this would not be the end but they would be ok for now. They would come looking for them, and he would be ready this time.

"Oh Shit Mathew your bleeding everywhere! What do I do?"

"Alicia,"

Katie was yelling at her now as she was driving the boat, she may have looked like a girly girl but I guess she had been in this life style long enough to know how to take care of herself.

"Here,"

 Katie was handing Alicia a part of her shirt from the bottom hem. "Put this around his leg really tight up above the bullet wound, it will help stop the bleeding. Put your hands together on top of each other and put as much pressure on the wound as you can."

Alicia did as she was told and Mathew groaned rather loudly at the pain from the pressure.

"I'm sorry Mathew" and let some pressure off but Mathew put his hand on top of hers and pressed giving her the silent ok to remain applying pressure, as much as he was in pain he knew she had to stop the bleeding. The bullet could have hit a major artery in his leg and he would bleed out before they ever got back to the main island if she didn't slow down the bleeding.

Once at the dock Mathew was going in and out of consciousness. Alicia was still applying pressure when Hank showed up at the dock and was asking what happened while pulling Mathew from the boat.

Katie explained the whole story to hank in the room adjoining, while the doctor saw Mathew. Hank had the doctor come to the hotel and see Mathew there; the hospital was an open target if the cartel was looking for them already, which they probably were. They took Alicia's name off the books and put them in a room that had been registered in someone else's name.

The doctor came out to talk to Alicia, Hank and Katie. He has lost a lot of blood but I was able to get the bullet out, he was very lucky it did not hit any major arteries. He should be up and running in a few days if I know Mathew.

Hank and Katie resumed their conversation while Alicia went into the other room to see Mathew.

"Mathew" He was in and out with the morphine that the doctor had given him.

"Mathew, I am so sorry I got you into all of this. I do not know how my life became so screwed up all of a sudden. I can't express how sorry I am, I don't know what to do, I…. have fallen in love with you Mathew."

Alicia was holding Mathews hand and laying her head on the side of is bed when he squeezed her hand, Alicia looked up and he was looking down at her.

"I thought you would never own up to your feelings about me, maybe I should have gotten shoot sooner. He smiled at her, she smacked his shoulder, and he groaned.

"Oh crap Mathew I'm sorry, but you deserved it."

Mathew tried to scoot up in the bed to sit up a little and he patted the side of the bed, Alicia stood up and gently slides in beside him careful not to make any big movements and hurt his leg. Lying down beside him, she put her head on his shoulder and kissed his cheek, not believing how happy she was, given the circumstances.

"Alicia"

Alicia looked up and smiled at Mathew "yea"

"Alicia, I have loved you since the first time you walked onto that dock and asked me about the trip. You were astounding and made me have butterflies like a fifteen year old school boy in love for the first time."

Mathew motioned to Alicia and she leaned up and kissed him lightly, the first kiss knowing she was loved, really loved. It was the best feeling in the world and she never wanted it to end. Then she remembered the last couple of days and wondered how they could ever just be happy when her past had come back to bite her and she did not even know why. Listening to him breath so steady and even she drifted to sleep and didn't wake up until Hank barreled into the room the next morning talking about something to do with a cabin and hiding out and who knows. She just wanted to stay with Mathew and not ever have to leave this room.

Alicia woke up to hear Hank and Mathew talking about what they should do about the cartel.

Alicia got up and went into the bathroom to wash her face and brush her teeth. She noticed that hank and Mathew were arguing and then heard the door slam closed.

Alicia came out of the bathroom,

"Mathew what is going on, are you fighting with Hank?"

"Alicia, everything is fine, we just disagree on how to proceed given the circumstances."

"Did he say where Katie is, did she tell him anything. Why she was with those people in the first place?"

"No, only what happened once you got there, nothing before that."

"Do you know where she is? I want to talk to her."

"I believe she is in the adjoining room but I'm not sure. Hey Alicia, don't probe too hard. I know you want to find out what happened to her and where she has been but you will push her away if you demand answers. Let her come to you, it might take a while but you will get your answers soon enough."

"Ok"

"Hey, Alicia"

She turned to look at him before going to look for Katie "yes"

"I love you" Alicia smiled and left the room.

Now that Alicia had left the room and Mathew was to him self again, he opened the laptop Hank had brought him earlier and started writing an email to his friend in NYPD.

"Hey, you will not believe what has happened here in the last few days' man. I think I am going to need some major help, I thought you might be able to get some of your contacts in the FBI a call. We have major Intel on a big Cartel leader here on one of the islands. Katie, Alicia's long lost foster sister just happened to be involved with Juan the leader, I do not know to what extent she is not saying much but I know she knows more than she is saying. They had Alicia and some stuff went down, and now they will be looking for us. I can't handle them on my own; I'm going to need your help."

"MATHEW.....MATHEW"

Alicia came running in the door holding a piece of paper crying.

"Mathew she left, she said that she was too much of a liability for us, that as long as she was here he would look for here. Mathew I think she went back

to him, how could she do that? How could she live with a killer? I don't understand…"
Mathew sat up a little higher and told Alicia to bring him the letter.

"Dear Alicia, I'm sorry to just leave like this but I have to go back. I know now that you did not just leave me when we were kids but I still need more answers and I do not think I can handle
They right now, too much have happened and I am not the kid you knew. I do not even know who I am but what I do know is that if I was to stay here with you, he will hunt you down and kill you. Your only shot of getting away from him is for me to go back; I will come up with some excuse to why I left with you. Something for his benefit, he will believe me. He might be a killer but he takes care of his own and he loves me. Maybe someday we will meet again and we can get to know each other without something hanging over our heads. I have always dreamed ever since I was a little girl that my big sister would come and rescue me, and you did. I just cannot stay; it is for your own protection. Go away from here Alicia and never look back, we will find each other again someday."

Mathew put the letter down and looked up at Alicia

"I'm sorry baby but you have to respect her decision to leave, she is trying to protect you"

"But Mathew I am her big sister, I should be protecting her not the other way around."

"I know baby but you have to let her go for now, I promise you we will find her and bring her back but we have to wait, we can't do it on our own. These people have way more resources than we have right now, we cannot fight them alone Alicia. We need to wait it out for a few days until we can get a plan together and I can get some help out here from the states. Try not to worry about Katie; I don't think he will hurt her."

Chapter 18
Two weeks later.......

"Alicia, can you come in here for a second?"
Alicia walks in from outside on the veranda in her bathing suit.
"Yea"
"I want you to read something"

Mathew,

Thanks for calling me in on the info for the cartel; I told you I would let you know when something happened. We were finally able to catch them in the act of drug trafficking. We caught them with 328 million in cash and drugs, not to mention the guns and all the evidence we were able to get on several murders over the past few years. Although we did not get Juan, I doubt he will resurface anywhere anytime soon; we have way too much on him. We did however get his supplier and the people that were working the closest with him. Let Alicia know that we found Katie and because she went willingly with you two off the island we were able to give her immunity contingent on her testifying on the cartel members and giving us all we need to put Juan away if he ever does resurface. She will be in witness protection and will not be able to communicate with anyone until the trials

are over. It could take up to two years for all of the case we have to go to the grand jury. Tell Alicia I am sorry but that is the way it has to be to protect Katie. After that's over, I will see what I can do to get them some time together again. As for the two of you, I hope you have had fun in Barbados on the FBI's dime. Bad news their money has run out, yall are safe, so enjoy your flight back home.
Oh yeah one more thing, that guy Nick-Alicia's ex boyfriend. We found him on the island when we were searching it for the cartel. He was shacked up in the temporary shelter you had built for Alicia's research project. Apparently, he is the one that blew up your boat, we linked him by fingerprints. The bad news is that all we got him on so, he wont be in the clink for very long so keep your eyes and ears open.

"I'm happy that it's over, but I hate that I can't see or talk to Katie. I am relieved that she is ok and is not going to be punished for her involvement. I just wish I had had the chance to get to know her a little. So what happens now?"
"As far as I am concerned you can't go back to your apartment, Nick knows everything about your life and like he said he won't be down for long, he might come after you again someday. You need to change up your habits and find somewhere else to

live. You're lucky you can do your job based from just about anywhere right?"

"Yes, but where would I go?"

Mathew pulled Alicia to his side and very slowly
got down on one knee, he was still sore from the
gunshot.
Holding both of Alicia's hands in his own he kissed
each one and simply said, "Alicia Marry Me!!"
Alicia got on her knees in front of him and said
"yes"

Acknowledgments

All the credit for the motivation and support goes to my husband and boys. My husband always believes in me and supports me no matter how crazy the idea. I have always loved writing but didn't do it until he convinced me I could. So here it is, I hope that everyone that reads this book will get some enjoyment out of it.
Thanks for giving me the chance and look for my next book.

www.ingramcontent.com/pod-product-compliance
Lightning Source LLC
Chambersburg PA
CBHW070917130626
46555CB00001B/178